A Deadly Agent

A Deadly Agent

Susan R. Sweet

VANTAGE PRESS
New York

FIRST EDITION

Copyright © 1996 by Susan R. Sweet

Published by Vantage Press, Inc.
516 West 34th Street, New York, New York 10001

Manufactured in the United States of America
ISBN: 0-533-11971-5

Library of Congress Catalog Card No.: 96-90241

0 9 8 7 6 5 4 3 2 1

To the Lord above; my loving husband, whose faith has kept me going; and my two sisters, Lesley and Vicki, who have supported me throughout my writing of the entire book.

A Deadly Agent

I

Penny stood at the railing staring at but not seeing the ocean. The twinkling stars and full moon cast their glow across the water. Looking past the picturesque scene before her, the young woman reflected upon the events of the previous months leading up to this voyage. It had only been eight months since her dad, the center of her universe, had died. As the gentle midnight breezes softly whipped the hair around her neck and face, she once again felt herself being drawn back to when her mother died. She had been thirteen at the time; and although her mother's death had been a blow, she hadn't felt the overpowering grief, the total devastation that had consumed her dad.

Her father, a writer, had withdrawn into himself, not letting anyone, including Penny, penetrate the wall of grief he built around himself. Her mother had contracted a rare form of cancer. Over a period of a brief two years, Penny and her father had watched the cancer slowly eat away at her mother's body. The illness had transferred the once healthy, beautiful woman into a small, childlike creature. Her dad had adored her mom and his spirit had died with her.

Now, looking back, Penny didn't understand why she hadn't been as grief stricken when her mom died as she now was from her father's death. She had loved her mother and felt her loss, but her feelings toward her mom still baffled her somewhat. She readily acknowledged to herself being much closer to her dad.

Penny and her dad had enjoyed life—fishing, hunting, and, her favorite, horseback riding. He had spent a lot of time teaching her to ride the horses they both loved. Fishing and hunting had taken a little longer. Penny wrinkled her nose at the memory of baiting her first hook. She had hated it, but known it was necessary to be able to share these moments with her father. He'd also taught her how to enjoy reading by totally losing herself in a book and actually becoming one of the characters in the story.

As she was an only child, her dad had spoiled her, she knew, but her mom hadn't seemed to mind and had encouraged their close relationship. Penny had tried to fill the void her mother left, but it just wasn't enough for her dad. Aunt Lesley had come down from Maine, moved in, and taken charge. She was the only relative Penny knew on either side, and she had grown to love and depend on her very much.

Almost a year after her mother died, and months of her dad's nearly grieving himself to death, a friend of his had told him about an estate being sold for taxes. As a favor, her dad had gone with him to look at it. For the first time in well over a year he had actually become excited and shown a little spark of life. After raving and ranting to Penny and Lesley for what had seemed like hours about how beautiful the place was, he'd also informed them that he had purchased it on sight, naming it "MaGrath's Paradise."

The next day they had driven out to see this "Paradise." It was as beautiful as her dad had promised. One hundred and fifty acres, back in the woods, on the outskirts of a quaint little town called Cedar Cove in northern Florida.

The house was huge. It had two stories and was log-cabin style, with decks that encircled the whole first and second stories. From the minute they saw it, Penny and Lesley had loved the place.

There were four bedrooms, each one with its own bath and a gorgeous view. Penny had picked the one looking down on a small pond and Les had chosen the room directly across the hall.

Her dad had started to write again after the move and, in a relatively short time, had another best-selling novel.

Everything was just starting to get back to normal when he began experiencing frequent painful headaches. The doctors had diagnosed them as a cluster-type headache and explained that there was nothing they could do for him except give him pain killers. The headaches had begun occurring more frequently, two and three times a week for several months, totally disabling him. It had been quite a welcome surprise when they had suddenly stopped.

She and her dad had started spending more and more time with each other. He had stocked the pond under her window with catfish, bass, and bream, and their daily horseback rides had resumed. On their last morning together, they had made plans to go fishing, her dad betting a new riding outfit that she would catch the biggest fish.

Waking before him as usual, Penny had dressed and gone downstairs. After fixing a pot of coffee, she had gone back upstairs to wake her father. Upon entering his bedroom and not finding him there, she'd gone downstairs into his study. He had been working on another book, and sometimes worked there all night. She's found him slumped over the typewriter. At first she'd thought he was asleep and had tapped him on the arm. When there was no response, she'd looked closer. She'd then noticed his color wasn't good and his skin felt cold to the touch. Screaming for her aunt and running from the room was the last thing she remembered before blackness descended.

They'd taken him away in the ambulance, while she and her aunt had held each other and cried. The doctors had said her dad had had a cerebral hemorrhage, which meant he had died instantly, not suffering like her mom. That knowledge had given her a little peace.

He had been buried beside her mom in a small gravesite funeral, following instructions his lawyer, Mr. Hiram Donner, had assured them were her dad's.

The following week the will was read, and it revealed that he had left everything to Penny. A sizable lifetime income had been established for her Aunt Les, who had also been made trustee over Penny's inheritance until she turned twenty-one, only four months away.

Shivering, Penny was torn back to the present. She still couldn't understand why there had been no autopsy and why the burial had been so rushed.

Realizing how cold and damp it now was on deck, she returned to her cabin, which was warm and cozy. Suddenly very tired, she decided to go to bed. Walking over to the full-length mirror, she absently noted the light auburn hair, more like her Aunt Les's than her mom's. Her eyes were dark brown, almost black, and she had a creamy smooth, flawless complexion, full mouth, and straight nose, just a little on the large side, which she supposed came from her dad's side of the family. She was actually five foot eleven and weighed normally between 190 and 200 pounds.

Painfully shy and overprotected, she had gone out on a few dates, but had never been serious about anyone. Penny, her dad, and Aunt Les had virtually lived in seclusion. She had always had a tutor and had graduated at home a couple of years ago in a small family ceremony. Their lifestyle was private, and this had really prevented Penny from forming friendships with kids her own age. That hadn't bothered her before, but now she felt entirely alone.

Throwing herself on the bed, Penny was finally able to release all the pent-up grief of the last few months and cried herself to sleep.

Waking a couple of hours later, Penny splashed some cold water on her face. Noticing her swollen eyelids, she put ice in a washcloth and draped it across them. As she relaxed and waited for the compress to do its trick, she once again went back in time to the eight months that had passed since her dad's death.

There had not been a lot of changes. She and her aunt had greeted each other at meals and sort of just floated around the place. Penny had spent a lot of time in her dad's study, as it made her feel his presence a little more. That's where Aunt Lesley had found her the morning she came in and announced that they were going to Australia. That conversation was still very clear in her mind.

"Penny, we have family in Australia who want us to come and visit." Holding up her hand to silence her niece's very verbal objections, Les had continued. "I realize you have never met them and have been through a lot of turmoil in a short period of time, but we are both just wallowing in our grief. A change of scenery and the support of family will help us get through this."

Penny once again objected, but was ignored. Les had reserved passage for Monday and here they were.

At first Penny was terrified. Why, she had never been out of the state, much less the country. Just who were these uncles and cousins who, before now, no one had bothered to mention? She wasn't looking forward to being yanked out of her safe haven into God knows what. Well, she had made up her mind not to go and that, Penny thought, was that. Boy, had she grossly underestimated her aunt's determination to get them away from the past and get started on a new future. Penny couldn't help but smile at the memory and once again went to sleep.

II

Waking up the next morning, still lying across the bed with a now cold, soggy cloth on her face, Penny jumped up, showered, dressed, and went up on deck. She looked out over the ocean, thankful she had been coerced into coming. Today was the last day of their voyage and they would reach Australia.

She had to admit that the ship itself was certainly nothing she had ever imagined. Les had been completely right in making her come. She chuckled as she recalled her stubborn aunt packing everything, with her all the while saying she wasn't going. Realizing Aunt Les was serious, even threatening to leave her alone at the house, Penny had quickly changed her mind. So here she was, really enjoying herself, and feeling just a little guilty at having given her aunt such a hard time.

They were rapidly approaching port, and she looked up in awe at the scene before her. The ocean was the bluest she had ever seen. Dolphins were jumping beside the ship. There were silver fish just under the surface of the water—hundreds of them—giving off shimmering rays of light as the sun shone through the water and reflected off their bodies. It was the most awesome spectacle she had ever seen. *If only Dad could be here,* she wished.

As the ship docked, Penny noticed a black station wagon. The man leaning beside it, looking very impatient, she guessed was in his late twenties. He had sandy blond hair, kind of long and curly at the ends. His piercing blue eyes at this very minute were staring a hole in her, making her drop her eyes and blush when she realized she had been rudely staring at him. She saw her aunt run over and get pulled into his encircling arms. His smile transformed his sour-looking features into an arrestingly handsome face.

Penny walked slowly down the gangplank and toward them cautiously, not wanting to impose on the happy reunion. She felt like an intruder. Seeing her niece's hesitation, Les motioned impatiently for her to join them.

"Penny, I want you to meet your cousin Devin."

Penny held out her hand.

"Glad to meet you," said Devin, taking her hand in his and openly appraising her.

"My, you're a tall one. You look just like Uncle Zack, or rather, what I can remember of him. Looks like she's got your hair, Les," he said, releasing Penny's hand but keeping his eyes on hers.

Penny shifted from one foot to the other. She'd never had anyone look at her like that. She had to listen closely to understand what was being said, as he talked in what she assumed was an Australian dialect. Clearing her throat and nodding her head, she tried to hide the tell-tale embarrassing red creeping up her neck.

"Well, let's get going. We have a two-hour drive ahead of us yet and we don't want to be caught by the dark. It's the rainy season, the 'wet' as we call it, and a lot of the roads are under water. I want to be able to see where I'm going."

He threw their luggage into the back of the station wagon and got into the driver's seat. Penny got in the back and her aunt in the front. She had a chance to study Devin without his being aware of it. He and Les were talking a mile a minute; and from the bits and pieces she could catch, things weren't going very well for Devin and his family. She really couldn't hear much with the wind blowing her hair around her face and whistling in her ears, but she was afraid to ask him to put the window up a bit. What she did notice was that he was very tan, had large shoulders, and a scar on his right cheek, which, she thought, only enhanced his good looks. His eyes were a mesmerizing blue. It felt really weird to be related to this man. Probably a good thing through, she surmised, feeling once again the familiar hot flush stain her cheeks.

They were approaching a rickety-looking bridge, when Devin started cussing. "Damn! We're going to have to speed up. The river is rising fast."

He put his foot on the gas and the car lurched forward. Penny's knuckles were white from grasping the seat. They sped across the bridge at a breakneck speed, bouncing and swaying recklessly. She felt a scream in the back of her throat but held it back.

Les was a little pale herself, but apparently a lot steadier than Penny. She turned around and looked at the frightened girl. "Don't worry, Pen. Devin knows these roads like the back of his hand. There's nothing to be afraid of."

"The hell there isn't!" Devin contradicted her. "If we don't get over the next bridge before the river crests, we will be right smack in the middle of the river. If you know any prayers, we could use them about now."

Penny bit her lip to keep back the tears that were stinging her eyes. She could see Les had clasped her hands together in her lap, causing the knuckles to turn white. For the next hour they strained their eyes, watching the progress of the rising water beside them. It seemed like they were going a hundred miles per hour. Devin was intent on the road in front of him and all conversation had come to a halt. The sun was starting its decline and Penny was terrified that they wouldn't make it. Then she saw the bridge ahead of them. Water was at the top and some was spilling over onto the bridge itself. Sweat was popping out on Devin's forehead. She could see he was contemplating the rise of the river to their crossing.

"We have no choice. We can't go back and if we stay here, we'll drown. Hold on. It's going to be a little rough."

Devin started across the bridge at a snail's pace. Penny wanted to scream at him to go faster. They would be washed off the bridge. Had he lost his mind? Slowly they made their way across, Devin moving the steering wheel left and right as the tires slid back and forth. Penny closed her eyes and listened to the roar of the river.

Please, God, let us make it, Penny said in a silent prayer.

Opening her eyes she saw they were over halfway across. More water was washing over the bridge. Les was now trembling in the front seat, and Penny moved forward to put her hand on her shoulder. Les leaned back against the seat. They stayed in that position the rest of the way across. When they reached the other side, Devin continued on for about two hundred feet, then braked the car and looked at both women.

"I've done that many times, and every time it scares the hell out of me. Sorry you had to go through this."

Penny looked back at him and was overwhelmed at the dazzling smile he was giving her. All she could do was mumble, "That's okay; I'm fine," and look down again quickly.

"Well, let's get going. We have about twenty-five more miles, and we'll be home."

Once again they all settled back in their seats, relaxed and silent for the rest of the trip.

"We're here."

Penny leaned forward and looked out the windshield. She saw what was the exact replica of "MaGrath's Paradise," but on a much larger scale. Now she knew why her dad had fallen in love with the place she called home. It must have reminded him of his birthplace here.

On the trip over, Les had told her a lot about the family history, filling in the void about her relatives, who previously were unknown to her. Uncle Dan had inherited the place from her grandparents, as he was the oldest and the only child still wanting to live in the house. She felt peace and tranquility fall over her. It was almost like coming home.

She saw a man standing on the porch and for a minute her heart flip-flopped. He looked just like her dad.

He strode out to the car, lifted Lesley up in the air, and twirled her round and round.

"It's been ten years, lass. Let me look at you."

Penny stood back and watched the touching scene before her. She barely let herself breathe, hoping she wouldn't break the spell. She hadn't seen her aunt look so young and happy in a long time.

"Put me down, you big galoot!" Les said, laughing.

Dan reluctantly eased his sister to the ground and looked across her shoulders. His eyes lit on Penny. All she could do was stand there and let the tears stream down her face. This man looked so much like her dad it was unbelievable. Dan was eight years older than her father, according to Les, but could have been his twin. He strode over to her and looked into her eyes.

"You look just like Zack, except that hair. Red just like your mom's and yours, Les. I'm glad to finally meet you, honey; and if you don't mind, I'd like to give you a big hug."

Penny didn't wait a second. She flew into her uncle's arms. It was so much like having her dad back, she could hardly stand it. He hugged her until she thought he would break all her ribs, but she didn't move. Penny felt alive again and looked back up into his eyes before giving him a kiss in return. She now knew they had done the right thing in coming here.

"Let's go into the house and let you freshen up. I know Devin, and I can just imagine how many bugs must have splattered on you through the windows. He never uses the air conditioner in the car. Says it's for wussies. Come on in. Myree has supper just about ready, so go get cleaned up and we'll eat."

The inside of the house was totally different from home. First of all, it made three of theirs. Devin led them up a large wooden staircase to two rooms side by side. Penny's room was done in the prettiest yellow buttercup wallpaper she had ever seen. The four-poster bed was enormous, with a pale yellow bedspread trimmed with cream lace on it. The rug was the palest yellow and a deep soft shag. The curtains matched the bedspread and gave the whole room a cheerful sunny appearance. Penny loved it.

Hurriedly shrugging off her clothes, she sank into the hot tub awaiting her. Before she realized what she was doing, she dunked her head under the water and totally relaxed her whole body. The tub was unusually long. The whole length of her body could spread out. She felt herself getting drowsy and immediately sat up, hurriedly lathered, and rinsed off. Not knowing where her suitcase would be, she piled her long hair on top of her head and pinned it up. Looking over the side of the tub, she spotted a cream-colored bath towel. Folding it around her, she stepped out of the tub. One of the suitcases was opened already, with a pair of tan shorts and a white peasant blouse laid out on the bed.

"I wonder who did that?" she mumbled to herself, but time was too short to speculate about it, so she dressed.

Looking into the mirror she saw how flushed the hot bath had left her and was pleased at the results. She normally used very little makeup and decided to use nothing but a little lip color. Leaving her hair pinned up, as it was still wet, she started down the stairs.

Penny looked around and saw that the staircase was centered in the middle of a large foyer. To the left was a huge dining room, with double swinging doors going into what she supposed was the kitchen. To the right was the largest room she had ever seen. On the far right wall was a beautiful rock and stone fireplace. All the furniture was wood and leather. It smelled of pipe tobacco and the outdoors. She could envision her dad relaxing in here. Uncle Dan, Aunt Lesley, and Devin were already in the dining room, talking.

"Are you going to stand up there all night, lass?" her Uncle Dan called out. "We're powerfully hungry and past ready to eat. Myree has been cooking all day, and I, for one, am going to do this feast justice." He dug a large fork into the plate of food before him, leaving no doubt he meant what he said.

Penny ran down the rest of the steps and joined everyone at the table. She couldn't remember ever seeing so much food in her life. There had to be at least three different kinds of meat, four bowls of various kinds of potatoes, a huge salad, vegetables unrecognizable to her, wine, and fresh baked bread. The smells were making her mouth water and her stomach growl.

Her uncle put down the fork and bowed his head. "For this food we give thanks. Amen." Grinning, Dan looked at the startled expression on Penny's face. "We don't waste unnecessary time on small chit-chat here. Too much to do and not enough time. Dig in, dig in," he urged as he attacked his own plate.

A petite woman entered with still more overflowing bowls of food.

"Lesley, you remember Myree, don't you?" Dan asked.

12

Her aunt got up, went around the table, and gave the small woman a huge hug. "I didn't know if you were still here or alive for that matter. You must be a hundred years old by now," teased Les.

Myree smiled and hugged her back. "I'll be eighty-two in December, young lady, but I'm as spry as I always was and just as capable of taking care of this family as I was at twenty. Now enough of this gibberish. Eat this meal before it gets cold and I get riled."

"Penny, I want you to meet Myree, Mom to us all."

The little old woman came right up to Penny's face and looked her over. "I wet-nursed your father and raised him up to a fine, strapping young man. He broke my heart when he left for America. Wrote me regularly, you know. I've known you since the day you were born. He was so proud of you." Tears in her eyes, she gave Penny a surprisingly strong hug.

Penny smiled back. "I'm glad to meet you too."

Her dad had never mentioned anyone over here and now she was curious as to why. Appetite overcame curiosity however and she started eating with relish. The food was different, but delicious. There was one meat that tasted like beef in a thick, rich gravy, ham sliced with pineapples and brown sugar syrup over it, and a platter of what she knew was fried catfish. There were mashed potatoes, potatoes broiled in butter, potatoes scalloped with cheese, and baked potatoes. The vegetables were corn, peas, tomatoes, and small carrots, all cooked in different sauces. She passed up the salad only because there was no more room on her plate. Listening to the hum of voices all around her, Penny continued to savor the wonderful meal before her. All of a sudden she realized the talking had stopped and everyone was looking in her direction. Blushing uncontrollably, she looked to her aunt for the reason.

Les laughed and, smiling at her, explained. "Dan just said you remind him of your father."

"He would get lost in the food at suppertime," Dan added. "Couldn't get one word from him until the meal was finished." He chuckled and everyone went back to eating and talking once again.

Penny paid more attention to the conversation going on around her, not wanting to be the center of attention for any reason again. Once the main course was finished and the dishes had been removed by some young boys, Myree came into the dining room with a huge chocolate cake. Chocolate was her favorite, but she just couldn't imagine where she was going to put it, as stuffed as she was.

"This cake is specially made for you, Penny. Les told me it was one of your favorites." Myree set the cake in front of her and held up the knife.

Seeing no escape, Penny accepted the first piece and lifted the fork to her mouth. It was the lightest cake she had ever tasted. The chocolate frosting was like eating mousse, rich but also light. The cake was gone before she knew it. What a wonderful meal.

They all pushed back their chairs and started into the living room. The fireplace had been lit, making it cozy and warm. Penny's eyelids were getting very heavy, but she forced them open. Uncle Dan was looking at her with a question in his eyes.

"Excuse me, did you say something?" Penny asked.

"I was just asking you if you want to go lie down. It's been a long day, I know, especially the trip here. Devin told us about the scare you all had coming here. The roads out this far are treacherous this time of year." Dan put his hand on her shoulder.

"I have to admit, it's hard to keep my eyes open," Penny answered, yawning.

14

Her uncle bent down and gave her a kiss on the forehead. "Go on to bed then, child. Get a good night's sleep. Our reunion can wait till morning."

Penny started up the staircase to her room. It felt like every bone in her body was aching. She didn't believe she had ever been this tired in her life. She put on her nightgown, slid between the cool sheets, and went immediately to sleep.

III

She awoke the next morning, disoriented, then remembered where she was. The sun was streaming through the window, birds were chirping, and the sound of some kind of animal, unfamiliar to her ears, was in the background. Getting out of bed, she crossed over to the double doors and stepped out onto the decking. Looking into the distance, she could see what looked like a massive river of white. She had never seen anything like it. Men were on horseback and a couple of strange-looking dogs were barking and running beside them. Looking right below her, she noticed Devin when he shouted at the closest man on horseback.

Realizing she was still in her nightgown, she drew back, but not before Devin had turned around, looked up, and caught her eye. She withdrew into the room, cheeks scarlet with embarrassment. No one had ever seen her in her night clothes before, except , of course, her aunt and Dad. How was she going to face Devin?

A knock at her door startled her. As she turned around, a young woman, not much older than herself, entered the room with a tray of tea and biscuits.

"Your uncle and aunt have already left to oversee the sheep herders this morning and didn't want to disturb you. They sent me up with this and to help you get ready for today. By the way, my name is Megan."

Penny smiled at the young girl, while sitting down in the rocker by the double doors. Megan came over and placed the tray on her lap and started straightening the bed.

16

Talking as she worked, she told Penny she was Myree's great-granddaughter and had lived there all her life.

By the time she had finished making the bed and laying out clothes for the day, Penny knew quite a bit about her uncle's home. The white river she had seen earlier were sheep. Her uncle and Devin's main livelihood came from the sheep they raised and sold. A mysterious sickness was killing off quite a few of the herd, and no one could identify its origin. If the cause wasn't tracked down soon, the ranch could be in jeopardy.

After Megan had finished her chores and gone, Penny hurriedly dressed, left her room, and bounded down the stairs. Seeing no one in sight in the dining room or living room, she went on out the front door. The porch ran the whole length of the house. Rocking chairs that looked well used lined it. The sounds of bleating sheep drifted back to her as the herd moved farther away. The surrounding yard was alive with men working on fences and in the barn to the left. On the right was what looked like a second main house, but on a much smaller scale.

While she was looking at it, a man came around the side. He was about the same age as Devin it seemed, only he had jet black hair, which was worn much shorter than her cousin's. He threw up his hand in a wave of greeting and she waved back. He walked right up to her with a wide grin across his face. His two front teeth were slightly spaced, which only added to his rugged good looks. His eyes were between green and hazel in color, and he had the longest eyelashes she had ever seen.

"Hey! I'm Kurt, the foreman," he said, introducing himself. "You have to be Penny. Your uncle wanted me to bring you out to meet them for lunch. I do believe you'll need some britches instead of those shorts though," he said, chuckling. "We'll be on horseback for a couple of hours."

17

Excited at the prospect of getting to travel by horseback, Penny told him she would be right back and nearly flew back up the steps to change her clothes. When she came back down with her leather riding pants and shirt on, Kurt gave a low whistle.

"My, you fairly take my breath away, lass."

"Thanks," Penny murmured, pleased but not really sure of how to take the compliment. No one except her family had ever told her she was good looking and, well, this was quite a bit different. She had to admit to herself that she liked it.

"Got a fairly spirited filly for you to ride named Sugar. Your aunt said you were quite the horsewoman. Hope she's not too high-strung for you."

"I can ride a horse very well. My dad taught me when I was five, and I've been riding ever since," said Penny.

"Good, then you'll be able to also enjoy the scenery out to the camp. You'll notice a lot of the ranch is under water, but we'll be going out to the high and dry country this afternoon," said Kurt, as he hauled himself up on a big black stallion.

Penny followed suit, lifting herself up onto Sugar's back.

"How many acres does my uncle own?"

"Seventy-five thousand, more or less," answered Kurt. "Used to own twice this, but he had to sell off half of it about five years ago when the drought nearly killed off all the sheep. It's been a long, hard fight back. Come on, let's ride," he said, as he darted forward.

Penny rode after Kurt, looking right and left as they went, the breeze whipping her auburn tresses out from under the scarf she had tied around her hair. If anyone had been watching, they would have been hard put to separate the woman from the horse, for they looked so much like an extension of one another.

Mile after mile rolled by as they rode on and on. Kurt would look back at her every once in a while to make sure, she supposed, that she was still there. After what seemed like hours, he slowed down to a canter. She caught up and brought herself to his side. They rode together in silence for another mile or two, when she spotted the camp ahead of them. Her aunt and uncle were bent over an open fire. He was stirring something in a big pot and her aunt was pouring coffee into mugs.

"You're just in time for lunch. Grab up a chair and sit down," said Les. She looked quite pretty, with her cheeks flushed and rosy from the fire.

Penny jumped down from her saddle and gave the reins of her mount to a man waiting for them. She was extremely sore and the last thing she wanted to do was sit in one of those hard aluminum chairs.

"I'll stand if you don't mind, Aunt Les. I'm a little tired of sitting just now."

"Fine, honey, suit yourself. Get a plate from that stack over there on the table."

Penny grabbed a plate and held it out to her uncle, only now realizing just how hungry she was. The stew he was ladling out looked delicious. Les was already eating hers. Kurt had continued on to the bunch of cowboys farther into the camp.

"How was your ride out here?"

"Wonderful," replied Penny and really meant it. It had been months since she had been on a horse, and she hadn't realized how much she really missed the thrill of riding.

"The scenery is so different from anything back home. I saw kangaroos and some strange-looking dogs Kurt said were dingoes. The air smells so fresh and everything is so open."

19

"Yes," agreed her Aunt Les. "I've really missed this much more than I ever thought I would. I almost feel like I'm eighteen again myself."

"I'm glad you enjoyed your ride, lass," broke in her Uncle Dan. "You'd better eat up though; we have many more miles to cover before we hit Ned's place."

Penny helped her aunt and uncle clean up the plates and cups. After they packed them away in the saddle bags, they all mounted up. Les and Dan led the way. Devin, joining them, paired off with Penny, and they both followed close behind. She hadn't seen Kurt since they entered camp and supposed he had already left with the hands.

There was no conversation as they were all concentrating on the passing scenery. The country they were riding through had a tough beauty. The trees and flowers were in contrasting harmony to each other. The kaleidoscope of red, green, and yellow foliage was unbelievable. When they finally stopped for a short rest, she asked her uncle how come there were so many flowers on land that was supposed to be grazing land.

"Why, lass, we haven't even reached the grazing land yet. The land we're crossing over here is your Uncle Ned's. He has no sheep or cattle. You'll meet him tonight. He has three thousand acres right smack dab in the middle of mine. All of it is still untouched, as you can see. He is a naturalist, a lot like your dad. We don't agree on a lot of things, but I can understand his love of the land. You'll see the wild flowers you're talking about all the way up to his door."

They had ridden for a couple of more hours when she saw a light in the distance. It just was dusk and the setting sun was beautiful. As they drew closer, she could see the outline of a house. She couldn't tell a lot about it, as it was getting quite dark, but she could see that it was about as large as Uncle Dan's. There were a man and woman standing on the front porch, and they started forward as the small group approached the house.

" 'Lo, Dan!" yelled the six-foot giant.

" 'Lo, Ned."

"Get down, get down. Come in. Thought you never would get here. Martha is about to have a fit to see Les again and meet this niece of ours."

They all dismounted and the horses were led away by the ranch hands. Ned and Dan shook hands and clapped each other on the back. Uncle Ned grabbed Lesley, kissing and hugging her until she looked like she was going to pass out.

"Let her go and give someone else a chance to say hello. Com'ere, Les, give me a hug." The short, squat woman enveloped Les in her arms, almost losing her in her abundant fleshy body.

Penny had never seen a woman as big as this aunt. *She must weight three hundred pounds,* she thought. Her aunt then focused on her and ambled her way.

"Well, lass, it's about time we got to meet ya. Welcome to our home."

Penny looked down and smiled into her aunt's sweet face, put out her arms, and gave her a hug. Her Uncle Ned was right behind her and she hugged him too. Everyone was talking at one time as they all climbed the stairs and went into the house.

They all entered a large hall with rooms to the right and left. Penny followed everyone into the dining room, which was on the left. There was a long oak table with at least twelve chairs. The entire surface was brimming over with food. The server was very short and brown in color, but somehow not like the colored people at home. *He must be an Aborigine,* thought Penny.

Her Aunt Martha showed her to the room off the dining area, which was a small washroom. "There, child. Freshen up and then join us before everything gets cold."

Penny splashed cold water on her face and washed her hands with the soap in front of her. It had a strange but pleasant scent and was very creamy. Pulling a comb through her hair and repositioning it atop her head, she reentered the dining room. Aunt Lesley patted the seat next to her and she sat down. All conversation stopped; everyone was looking at her.

"Penny, girl," said her Uncle Dan, "are you wondering yet why you were pulled from the boat to the wilderness?"

"Well, yes, I suppose so," replied Penny.

"We actually had this trip planned for later in the week; but four more of the sheep died yesterday, and I had to have Ned's help on this."

"I'm a botanist," broke in her Uncle Ned. "Dan thinks this strange sickness might have something to do with the plant life up on the northern pasture. We all hated to drag you about, but this is the MaGraths' livelihood and must come first. You understand, don't you, lass?"

"Of course," replied Penny. "Don't worry about me. I've enjoyed every minute of my visit so far. This has been a lot more interesting than sitting around, and it's been a long time since I've been on a horse. I've loved every minute of it," said a smiling, happy Penny.

"Great! Let's eat first and then we can all get acquainted properly," said her Aunt Martha, as she started passing bowls of food to her uncle.

"We're not formal here, as you can see. It's only Ned and me, since Kit, that's our son, moved out with his wife. You'll meet him and Kathleen before you leave."

They all concentrated on the meal in front of them, passing bowl after bowl of steaming hot food to each other.

Penny ate until she thought she wouldn't be able to breathe. *I'm going to gain one hundred pounds if this is what all mealtimes are like,* she thought.

"Let's go into the den," said her Aunt Martha, as she got up from the table. Everyone followed suit and pushed themselves from the table.

"Oh, my! I think I'm going to need someone to wheel me in," said Les, as she laughingly puffed out her cheeks and slowly dragged herself from the table.

"Come on, Sis, who do you think you're trying to fool? You could outeat all of us and the ranch hands when you were home," said Uncle Dan, laughing, as he came around the table, linked his arm through hers, and pulled her toward the door.

Penny felt a warmness inside as she watched the camaraderie flow between her aunt and uncle as they all walked into the den. This was a new experience for her, an only child, and she was enjoying it to the fullest.

The den was obviously a masculine domain. All the furniture was done in brown leather. The floors were bare polished wood, what kind she had no idea, but beautiful. No curtains hung at the big bay windows, which were on both sides of the room. A large-screen television took up the whole left wall, and an old wood rolltop desk was in the corner. It was very obvious that this was the living center of the house.

Finding a chair, Penny sat down and surveyed the people around her. Her Aunt Les, Uncle Dan, and Uncle Ned were apparently having a very serious discussion. As she studied their expressions, she was surprised to see the same furrow in the line above the eyebrows as her dad had when he was explaining a story line or giving her a lecture. How so much alike yet so different they all looked.

She couldn't believe, as she reflected on the events of this past week, just how much her world had changed in so short a time. She felt really alive, part of a family again, and her naturally curious nature was burning inside of her once more. Feeling a tap on her arm, Penny looked up to see her Aunt Martha smiling at her.

"You haven't heard a thing I said, have you, child?"

"I'm so sorry," said a remorseful Penny. "I'm bad about daydreaming. It drives Aunt Lesley crazy."

"That's okay. I'm guilty of doing the same thing myself," said her aunt. "I'm by myself a lot when your uncle's working. It's company to you to let your mind drift when you're alone. I was just asking you if you enjoyed your trip over."

"Oh, yes," came Penny's quick reply. "The ocean was beautiful, and the ship was like being in a floating hotel. The food was outstanding, and there was so much to do. I have to admit, I was really against coming over here, Aunt Martha, but Aunt Lesley knew what she was doing when she made me come." Stopping to catch her breath, she hesitantly continued. "Everyone is so nice. It's really strange, you know. Dad never talked about his family. I would ask questions now and then, but he would always put me off. I had the feeling that he left Australia under bad terms."

"That, child, is something you'll have to ask your uncles. I've been told I have a loose tongue, so I'll keep my mouth shut and out of the family closet, so to speak; but I have to say I'm not surprised your aunt hasn't told you anything. The MaGrath clan are a tight-lipped bunch of people. I wasn't raised that way though, being from a family with seventeen children. There was no time for secrets." Chuckling to herself, her aunt went through the door and back into the dining room.

Penny turned around and looked at her aunt and uncles still sitting with their heads together, talking and laughing. It was a cozy scene and made her feel good inside.

Her Uncle Dan looked up and caught her eye. "I don't know what's gotten into us, just a-jabbering and leaving you all to yourself. We're all a bunch a slobs with no manners."

Penny started to deny feeling left out, but her Uncle Ned broke in. "Guess you're wondering what kind of people invite you to come halfway around the world, take off, make you travel half the day in the heat and dust on horseback, then leave you to your own resources to keep yourself amused."

"Oh, no!" started Penny, but Uncle Dan threw up his hand, halting the denial.

"We're sorry to give you such a ramshackle welcome, but we are in the middle of what could be a disaster for the ranch. We're going to have to go farther up-country in the morning, your Aunt Les, Ned, and myself. Ned's going to bring his portable lab and do some testing on the grass, soil, and plants where the sheep have been grazing. Something's killing them; and if we don't find out what it is soon, it could mean the end of our ranch. Your Aunt Martha will be here with you, and rest assured, she'll more than welcome the company. Devin will also be around and about if you need him. Sorry to have to leave you, but this can't wait. The sheep are dropping like flies, and time's of the essence here."

"I'd like to come along, if I could," started Penny.

Les came over and put her arm around Penny's shoulders. "Pen, we'd like for you to come if it were under different circumstances, but we don't know what we're dealing with at this point. You aren't familiar with the outback and would only hold us back. We'll only be gone a week, maybe two, and I'm sure you'll enjoy yourself right here." With that said, her aunt and uncles went back to their chairs and their discussion.

Feeling a little hurt and somewhat puzzled, Penny turned around and started to go find her Aunt Martha. The little man called Ben met her just on the other side of the den door. He didn't speak but motioned for her to follow him. Aunt Martha came out of the dining room and, seeing Penny's hesitation, took her by the hand.

"Ben's going to show you to your room, Penny. He's a mute but understandable once you get to know him."

"Is he deaf, too?" asked Penny.

"Oh, no," her aunt said, laughing. "He can hear much better than any of us, sometimes too good!"

They followed Ben down the foyer through double doors into another smaller room with a staircase. Aunt Martha kissed her forehead. "See you in the morning."

Penny followed Ben up the stairs. At the top was a long hallway. She looked in both directions and saw several doors to what she supposed were all bedrooms. At the end of the hallway to the left she could see a massive wooden door. That would be the master bedroom, she assumed, as Ben led her to the third door on the right. He opened the door and stepped aside to let her enter. She went inside and was amazed at the transformation from the rest of the house.

The room was done totally in pinks and peaches. It was a perfect room for a little girl. There was a canopy bed in front of the window, with a peach top and matching spread. The carpet was peach and pink in a swirling design, with small throw rugs in both colors all around the room. A wooden dresser was on one wall, and a matching wooden dressing table with a mirror on the other wall. There was a door just past the dressing table, which, when she investigated it, turned out to be to a small bathroom.

She turned around to ask Ben about a change in clothes and saw that he had disappeared. Going back to the door and looking down the hallway, she saw that it was also empty. *Well, that's just great,* she thought. Not knowing that she wasn't going back to Uncle Dan's today, she had not packed any of her clothes. What was she going to sleep in tonight and, for that matter, wear for two weeks? Crossing the room, she opened the closet doors. It was full of shirts and slacks. She went back to the dresser and pulled open the drawers. It was also filled with nightgowns, underpants, bras, anything she could possibly need, and everything looked like it would fit her. *Boy, is this strange or what?* she thought. *I'm not the easiest size to fit. It looks like this room was ready made just for me.*

Penny sat down in the chair next to the bed and pondered over the day's events. If it wasn't for her Aunt Lesley being downstairs, she would be very uneasy about all this; but she knew her Aunt loved her very much and would never let any harm come to her. *I'm just overtired and letting my imagination run wild,* she thought.

Grabbing up a pretty white nightgown, she went into the bathroom, ran the tub as full of steaming hot water as her body could stand, and sank into it little by little. The heat was soaking into all the sore muscles she hadn't realized were aching until now. Not having been on a horse for months was really telling on her buns and legs. *Hopefully, Uncle Ned has some horses I can ride here,* she thought. *I have to get back into shape.* She dunked her head under the water, wetting her hair. It felt wonderful. She could feel her whole body relaxing.

She remembered when her mom would come into the bathroom at the old house, fussing about her daydreaming in the bathtub. She wiped her eyes and brought herself back into the present. *Enough of that, young lady! Feeling sorry for yourself isn't going to help anything.*

Standing up, she dried off, stepped out of the tub, slipped the nightgown over her head, and walked back into the bedroom. Crossing over to the windows, she looked out but could only see blackness. Not a star was out, and the moon couldn't be found. She had slipped beneath the sheets before realizing she had forgotten to turn out the light. She started to get back up, when Aunt Les came into the room.

"I see you've made yourself right at home. This is a pretty room, isn't it? I'm really surprised Martha let you have this one. It's been closed up, according to Ned, since Angela died."

"Who's Angela?" asked Penny, now wide awake with curiosity.

"She was Ned and Martha's oldest girl. Dan wrote your dad and me telling us about her death I guess three or four years ago. Actually, you remind me a lot of the pictures Martha used to send us. Your coloring is totally different though. She had black hair and an olive complexion, but she was tall and built a lot like you. Ned seems to think that your being here will help Martha a lot over the next couple of weeks."

"How did she die?" asked Penny, once again feeling a little uneasy.

"That was never really clear to your dad and I. It was something like what happened to your mom, a cancer, or some kind of disease, that took her fast. I've never questioned Ned or Martha on the phone or by letter. I didn't want them reliving her death all over again. Anyway, Martha had her room closed up until now, according to Ned. Wouldn't even let Kathleen or her brood in. I guess she's ready to let go now. But that's not what I came up here for, young lady. I hope you're not too hurt having to stay here. I really think you'll enjoy being with Martha, and I know Ned will feel a lot better with your being with her, too."

"It's all right, Aunt Les. I was feeling kind of bad earlier, but I understand. Besides, I like Aunt Martha. It'll be fun getting to know her and wandering around the land here. Are you leaving Sugar for me to ride?"

Suddenly Les's tone of voice changed. "Under no circumstances are you to go off by yourself! Do you understand?" her aunt half shouted at her.

"Why? I'm more than capable of taking care of myself," huffed Penny.

"Pen, you're not familiar with the country over here. Martha would be beside herself if anything happened to you in her care. Don't go anywhere without her or Devin with you, okay?"

Penny's earlier feelings of uneasiness started to come back. "Sure, if it's going to mean that much to you. I'll find something to do with my time," she said.

Les leaned down and kissed her cheek. "When all this is cleared up, I'll be able to explain things better to you and why all the precautions and secrecy. Until then, trust me. Now promise me, Pen."

"Okay, I promise," said Penny.

Les then turned around and, switching off the light as she left, closed the door. Lying in total darkness, Penny reflected back on the day's events. Never in her young life had she experienced this much adventure and mystery. Her natural curious nature and vivid imagination had her daydreaming all kinds of way out things when her eyelids finally closed and she fell into a deep, exhausted sleep.

She was dreaming her usual dream. Penny, her dad, and her mom were on the beach. Her mom wasn't sick in this dream, and they were all laughing and throwing sand at one another. All of a sudden, out of the corner of her eye, she could see a man. She had never seen him before,

29

but she knew he was dangerous. The man wasn't doing anything but looking at them, and she couldn't see his face very clearly, but he meant them harm. She could feel it. Her heart started beating very fast in her chest. She was trying to warn her dad and mom, but they were laughing and ignoring her frantic cries. She looked back at the man, but he was gone! Her heart was banging, and she was choking for air. Someone was trying to smother her!

She wasn't dreaming now. Struggling to get awake, she tried to open her eyes. Someone was standing over her; she could feel their presence. Terrified, she lay still, praying that the person couldn't see her eyelids fluttering. Ever so slowly she opened her right eye. Letting herself get accustomed to the darkness surrounding her, she looked to the side of her bed and up. Nothing was there. She listened, barely breathing, but could hear nothing. She opened both eyes wide, sat up in bed, and scanned the room. There were shadows all over the walls. She felt like screaming, but she didn't want to alarm everyone. What had caused the turn of events in her dream? She had had the same dream for years, always awakening with a sense of peacefulness inside. Never before had it turned into a nightmare.

Very much shaken, Penny lay back down and tried to calm herself. Her imagination must have really gone nuts! *I'll get up with Aunt Les and convince her I have to go with them. I don't like it here,* she thought. *It can't be much longer till dawn. I'll just stay awake until they get up.* With that resolved, Penny sat back up, got out of bed, and went over to the chair. Sitting down in it, she pulled the blanket she had taken off the bed around her, opened her eyes wide, and started humming to herself to keep awake.

IV

Penny awoke to the sun streaming in the window. Jumping out of the chair, she raced to the closet, grabbed a robe, and rushed out the door. Seeing no one in the hallway, she found the staircase and took the steps two at a time. Her Aunt Martha was just inside the dining room door when she hit the bottom of the stairs.

"Goodness, child, you going to a fire?"

After stopping in her tracks and looking at her aunt, Penny felt a little foolish. In the daylight, the demons of the previous night seemed a lot less fierce. "Have they gone?" she asked.

"Left a couple of hours ago, dear. Been up as long myself. Already had my breakfast. You want some?"

"Not right yet," Penny replied, "but a cup of tea sounds good."

"Ben, bring a pot of tea and a couple of cups in, please."

The little man nodded and left the dining room through the opposite door. In what seemed like a second, he reappeared with a steaming pot, two cups, a plate of biscuits, and a jar of jam.

Penny sat down at the dining table directly across from her aunt. As she spooned the jam onto the biscuits, she studied her as well as she could without appearing to stare at her rudely. She looked older than her Aunt Les but younger than Uncle Dan. From what little Megan had told her the previous morning, Ned was the youngest of her uncles. Aunt Les, the only girl, was next, then her dad. Uncle Dan was the oldest. Aunt Martha was very pretty and had beautiful black hair that was just beginning to turn silver. It looked like she had never had it cut, as it lay in waves all around her face and down her back. Her eyes were a very light blue, almost a gray color, and she was a lot shorter than Penny. Her aunt smiled back at her and broke into her observations with one of her own.

"You remind me a lot of my daughter, Angela, especially in her robe and gown."

"I'm sorry," started Penny, but her aunt waved her off, and continued. "Nothing to be sorry about, girl. When Ned told me you were coming, it was the right thing to do to clean all her clothes and ready the room for you. I believe Angela would have liked you staying there." Martha was blinking her eyes very fast and stopped to drink her tea.

"You don't have to talk about it if you don't want to, Aunt Martha."

"No, it's time, it's time," said her aunt. Then she looked past Penny into space and haltingly started to talk.

"It happened four years ago last week. I watched her take her last breath and wanted to die right then with her. She was my baby, you know, and had just turned twenty-two. She'd gotten sick about six or eight months before. Always been big and healthy, a lot like you, before that. We took her to one doctor after another. None of them could agree on a diagnosis, calling it one big name after another. I couldn't understand all the medical terms and words they used, but I do know I watched helplessly as my baby had one kind of treatment after another, like a human guinea pig. None of them did anything but make her suffer and get worse. Finally we'd had enough, so Ned and I brought her home to die. It only took six months from the time she got ill till she died. Just wasn't fair, it should have been me, not her. You know, they never could tell us what actually killed my baby, just guesses, all guesses, but she's gone all the same." Her aunt put her head in her hands and started sobbing.

Penny rushed around the table and put her arms around her, trying to comfort her as best she could.

"Look at me," said her aunt, as she straightened up and wiped her eyes. "Your first day here and I'm doing my darndest to ruin it. I'm sorry, dear, but you look so much like her in a way; guess it brought back memories." She then stood up and, catching Penny's shoulders, gave her a big hug.

"You'd best be getting dressed. There's a lot for you to see around here. Devin's coming back in less than an hour to show you some of the place. You'll need long pants and a long-sleeved shirt, as the bugs are quite numerous this time of year." With that said, she nudged Penny toward the stairs.

Having mixed emotions about spending the day with Devin, while leaving her aunt alone, Penny slowly mounted the stairs. She felt that if she was going to learn anything about this family, her Aunt Martha was the one person from whom she would get the most information. Slowly picking her way through the clothes in the closet, she chose an olive pair of pants and a tan long-sleeved shirt. She found she would have to wear her own shoes as her cousin's were slightly too small for her. She left her hair down, just combing out the tangles.

Coming down the stairs, Penny heard voices. One was her aunt's, but the male voice was unfamiliar to her. As she came into the den, a man brushed past her, nearly knocking her over. "Excuse me, ma'am," he said, as he ran out the front door.

"Who was that?" asked Penny.

"That was Frank. He's your uncle's handyman, lab assistant, and anything else you might want to call him. Your uncle sets quite a store by him. Appeared out of the blue several months ago and more secretive about his past than the MaGraths are. I don't trust him, although I don't quite know why. Never done anything to me, but there's just something about his eyes. Lord, hear me rambling on again. Your Uncle Ned is right; I talk too much." Laughing, her aunt came over to her and looked her over.

"Clothes just fit, don't they? I'm glad they do. Now let's go outside and see if we can scare up Devin."

Devin was riding up with the chestnut mare in tow as they stepped out on the porch. Throwing the reins to Penny, he asked, "You need a hand up?"

"No thanks. I can manage," replied Penny, as she hoisted herself up on the horse.

"Be back by noontime now!" yelled her aunt, as they trotted off.

Following Devin in silence, Penny got the feeling he would rather be anywhere else but riding with her. Pushing all thoughts out of her mind, she was determined not to let his hateful attitude ruin her morning. There were a lot of green stout trees she supposed were the gum trees Aunt Les had told her were so plentiful here. When she ventured to ask Devin, all she got was a nod of his head, affirming the fact. Determined not to ask him anything else, she concentrated solely on the scenery around her. It was like something out of a travel brochure. The riot of reds, yellows, and greens in the flowers was totally awesome and they seemed to be everywhere. The birds were as colorful as the plants. In the distance she could see hills and wondered if there would be snow at the top.

They rode in silence for what seemed like hours, when Devin finally slowed down and stopped beside a small stream. It seemed to be gushing out of a wall of stone. "We'll rest the horses for about twenty minutes, then we'll start back," he said.

"Fine," murmured Penny, as she eased herself off her mount. Untying the scarf from around her neck, she leaned down and wet it in the stream. Wiping the dirt from her face, she stole a glance at Devin. He was sitting on his heels, staring at the water.

"Did I do something wrong?" Penny ventured.

He looked up suddenly as if he were seeing her for the first time and slowly shook his head. "No. I guess I've been a real horse's ass to you and I apologize. I wanted to go on up to camp with Dad and Uncle Ned, but they wanted me to stick around and show you the landscape here. It's not your fault. My mind is on the sheep. I promise to be a real tour guide on the way back." With that said, he then turned the full force of his smile on her.

She was astonished once again to see the transformation in his features. *It's a good thing he's my cousin,* she was thinking, *or I think I'd be in a lot of trouble.* Charmed by his change in attitude, Penny warmed up to Devin and they carried on a constant conversation on the way back to the house. She learned that he had been born at his father's house and had never been anywhere else but the ranch. He was twenty-eight, unmarried, and his love for the ranch and the sheep totally filled his life.

They had almost made it back to the house when he abruptly stopped and, looking over at her, smiled once more. "Look, I'm really sorry once again for earlier. I've enjoyed the trip back very much. Dad says you like fishing, and if you'd like, we'll do some tomorrow."

Penny, having also enjoyed his company, was extremely light-headed about the prospect of spending tomorrow fishing with him. "That'll be great!" she said, and they both continued on to the house.

"See you 'bout five in the morning!" Devin shouted, as he continued on toward the stables with Sugar behind.

Penny smiled and nodded her head, then turned and went up the porch steps and on into the house. Once inside, Penny could smell her favorite food, hamburgers. She went into the dining room and found her aunt sitting at the end of the table.

"Hope you like burgers with cheese," said her aunt.

"I love them. How'd you know they're my favorite!"

"Seems we have something in common then; they're my favorite too. We don't have them much, mostly 'cause your uncle likes veggies and such; but when he's away, wellll, you know what they say. Hurry and wash up so we can eat. I'm starved," said Martha, as she started loading her burger with just about everything in sight.

Penny washed up hurriedly and came in and sat down. She liked her hamburger with just mustard and ketchup. After pouring these on her bun, she sank her teeth into the juiciest and, by far, tastiest hamburger she'd ever eaten.

"What is it about this place?" asked Penny. "Everything I've eaten here is so much better than home."

"Don't you know everything is supposed to be better when you're on vacation, child? Plus, of course, I'm the best cook ever, and my figure can confirm that fact."

"You do your own cooking?" asked Penny.

"Why do you look so astonished? What else is there to do out here? If I didn't cook, I'd just go crazy, and I really enjoy experimenting in the kitchen. When the kids were home, it was the happiest room in the house. Now I still cook, but a lot of fun's gone from it, you know what I mean?"

Nodding her head, as her mouth was full of food, Penny agreed.

"Today I really had fun preparing lunch for you. Les filled me in on some of your likes and dislikes after you went to bed last night. Hamburgers really are a favorite of mine so, as you can see, they came first. But on a more serious note, Penny. I'm really looking forward to what time we have together, getting to know one another and all. You'll find me easy to get to know. My main fault, however, is my mouth." Aunt Martha laughed softly and continued, "I really like to talk, so I hope you like to listen. Ned turns a deaf ear to me most of the time; and I've got to admit, I get on my own nerves sometimes."

Penny smiled at her aunt, liking her more and more with each passing minute. "I don't like to talk much myself. Dad always called me painfully shy. I do want to hear all about my new-found family. Everyone has been so loving and kind to me. So what I'm trying to say in a roundabout way is that I'll be glad to listen, and I don't believe you'll ever get on my nerves."

Both women looked at each other, smiled, and then concentrated on the meal before them, neither stopping again until everything was gone from their plates.

"Let's go into the den," said her aunt when they were finished. So Penny followed her lead into the cozy room.

"I can't believe I didn't notice the bookcase last night!" exclaimed Penny, as she glanced to the right when they entered the room.

"You have all Dad's novels and everyone else's for that matter, it looks like."

"Ned likes to read a lot at night and so do I," said Martha. "He and your dad didn't share the same interests, but he was sure proud of Zack's writing accomplishments. As you can see, he has everything your dad ever wrote that was published, of course. Like I said before, this is a strange family, but they're all proud of each other's achievements."

"Aunt Martha?" began Penny.

"Go ahead, child. I've been waiting for you to ask some questions ever since you got here," said Martha, sitting down in the brown leather recliner.

"Why didn't Dad ever come to visit here or any of you come visit us? I can't even remember Dad mentioning anyone in his family, except Aunt Les and Uncle Dan. Did Uncle Ned have a falling out with Dad? Was there bad blood between you all here and Mom maybe?"

"Slow down, girl. One question at a time," broke in Martha. "First of all, no, Ned and your dad did not have a falling out. Uncle Dan and your dad did. Yes, it had something to do with your mom. Look at me, I'm doing just what Ned was afraid I'd do in talking about it. I believe you're old enough to handle the truth though and keeping it all secretive and such makes it seem worse than it is, if you know what I mean."

Penny nodded, afraid that if she said anything it would interrupt or stop her aunt from talking.

"Polly, your mom, was the prettiest little thing you ever saw back then. Every man around these parts was plumb crazy about her. She and your Uncle Dan were dating while your dad was away at school and things were looking pretty serious when Zack came home for the holidays. From the beginning he couldn't take his eyes off her. She seemed to be the same way about him too, although they tried real hard not to let anything happen, her being practically engaged to Dan and not wanting to hurt him. So Zack went back to school, I mean college. He was twenty then, not a schoolboy.

"Polly's feelings toward Dan had changed by then, and things had started to cool between them. It was real hard on Dan. He couldn't understand why, and he continued to pursue Polly. Well, she just up and left one morning. Went to visit her cousin in England. Her dad told Dan that she had to get away and get her thoughts together.

"Dan about went crazy. Started drinking real bad. Let the ranch go to pot. Ned tried to talk with him, but he just got cussed at. So after a time, Ned just left him alone.

"About two years went by and the next thing we knew Zack wrote us he was coming home. Told us in the letter that we would all be surprised. Dan had straightened himself up and had put all his energy into the ranch. He was real excited at the idea of having Zack back home and planned a big welcome with all the family for him.

"Ned met Zack and Polly at the ship. Ned said you could have knocked him over with a feather when Zack told him he was married and to Polly no less. He knew there would be trouble back home when Dan found out, so he tried to convince your dad and Polly to stay in town until he told Dan.

"Well, that thoroughly pissed Zack off. Said there wasn't anything to break to Dan, said that Polly and his relationship had ended two years before. He felt Ned was building this all out of proportion. They all got into the truck and came to the house. I'll never forget the look on Dan's face when he saw Polly get out of the truck. He looked at Zack then back at her and shook his head like he was trying to clear his sight. He took the truck keys from Ned, jumped in, and took off. There must have been fifty people here, but you could have heard a feather drop.

"You can just imagine how hurt and embarrassed your dad was. He asked Ned if he could go on to our house. Then everyone, finally coming to their senses, rushed around congratulating Zack and Polly. They started hugging and kissing them and trying to get them to come on in the house. Your dad wouldn't have any of it. Said it appeared he wasn't welcome here and he didn't go where he wasn't wanted. So Ned, me, the kids, Zack, and Polly all loaded up into our truck. I was a lot smaller back then," Martha added with a smile. "Then we came on to the house here."

"What happened then?" asked Penny, not wanting her aunt to stop for a minute.

"Hold your horses, girl; I've got to have something to drink. My mouth is dry from all this talking. Ben! Ben!" The little man came running into the room.

"Bring us some tea, please," asked Martha.

Ben went out and in just a few minutes came back with a tea tray. Penny was amazed how fast he always was. After pouring the tea, he left, and her aunt settled back in the chair with her cup and continued.

"We were all so exhausted from the day's activities, and your dad and Polly from their trip, that we all went on to bed. The next morning Devin, who wasn't but seven or eight at the time, Myree, Lesley, and the foreman—Jim I believe his name was—pulled up with all Zack's belongings in the back of the truck. Your Uncle Dan had literally thrown everything out in the yard when he came home roaring drunk they said. They picked it all up and brought it here.

"Les was the most upset. She fairly idolized Zack, he being the closest to her and all, but it was Dan's house and she hadn't been able to reason with him. Zack and Polly stayed here about a week. He had a writing assignment for a big magazine over in the States. They had already rented a place over there and were eager to get started. We never saw Zack or Polly again. Lesley was the only one who went to America to see your dad. We talked to him and Polly from time to time, but Ned's work and the kids and all kept him busy here. Well, when Les called and told us Polly had died, Ned went straight over to Dan's. From what I gather from Myree, Ned blessed Dan up one side and down the other. Dan finally came to his senses and tried to call your dad, but too much time had passed I guess. Anyway, they never did speak to one another after that awful night.''

"Well, now I don't understand why he's so nice and loving to me," said Penny. "You would think nothing had ever happened."

"Penny, the day Lesley called and told Dan that Zack was dead, why, it was worse than the day he showed up with Polly. Dan about went out of his mind. He didn't drink though, but he came to the house and talked with Ned. They both got on the phone with Les and asked her to bring you over here. Les refused at first, I guess out of loyalty to your dad. About a month later, Dan called again. She then said she thought it would do you good to meet the family and get away from there for a while. So here you are. I hope this doesn't change how you feel about any of us," asked her aunt, watching Penny's face closely.

"No, I can't judge anyone by what happened years ago. Everyone has been wonderful to me, and I know Dad would have really appreciated that," said Penny.

"Good," said Martha, letting out a sigh. "I didn't think it would hurt your to know the story. Now, if you don't mind, child, I think I'm just going to close my eyes for a minute or two."

Her aunt leaned back in the recliner and was asleep in no time. Penny slipped from the room and went outside. It must have rained for everything was wet and smelled fresh.

Looking around the front and side of the house, she could see that the structure had to be quite old but in really fine condition. Going around the house into the back, she saw a garden meticulously clean of weeds. There were all kinds of vegetables in the beginning and ripe stages of growth. Ben came up from behind and startled her some-what, motioning for her to follow. Going past the garden

and down the lane, they came upon a pretty gazebo surrounded with the wild flowers she so admired around here.
It looked like a picture postcard. Ben motioned for her to
sit in one of the chairs. As she did, he made an eating gesture
and started back into the house. She surmised that he was
going to bring her something and settled back.

Sitting in the wooden chair, Penny looked all around
her. It was so different from her Uncle Dan's place, but not
unlike home. She became a little nostalgic thinking about
home, but broke that thought to sort out her feelings on all
she had heard today. One thing stuck out in her mind more
than anything. Apparently, her Uncle Dan had never married after his relationship with her mom, so—what about
Devin? She supposed her uncle must have been married
before he met her mom. *I'll have to ask Aunt Martha about
that when she wakes up,* she thought.

Looking up and around the wooded area, she spotted
a man standing against a tree. He looked vaguely familiar,
but she couldn't see his features very well. Ben was coming
back with a snack and after he placed it on the table in front
of her, she looked back up and over to the tree. The man
was gone. *Strange,* she thought, but didn't dwell on it as the
aroma of fresh-baked brownies drifted from the plate in
front of her. *Now I know why my aunt is so big. If I keep eating
so much, I'll certainly resemble her before I leave here.* With a shrug
and a little laugh, Penny devoured the brownies, then emp-
tied the glass of milk beside them.

The gazebo was cool, with a gentle afternoon breeze
flowing through it. Penny, sufficiently sated, was not extremely tired. Settling back into the comfortable chaise and
closing her eyes, she drifted off to sleep.

She was dreaming again, but this time she, her dad, and
Aunt Les were horseback riding. Everyone was laughing and

joking, trotting alongside each other, enjoying the country-side. Her dad and aunt fell back, telling Penny to go on ahead of them. Sensing that they had something to discuss, she increased her speed into a gallop. After a few minutes of a full gallop, she slowed down. When she came to a full stop and turned around to see how far back her dad and Les were, she was startled to see a figure on horseback following behind them. She turned back and raced as fast as she could toward them, trying to warn them of impending danger. She rode and rode, but they were getting no closer to her. The figure behind them was closing the distance between them. Now she was screaming at the top of her lungs and racing as fast as she could. Her dad and aunt looked up and both smiled at her. "No! No!" she shouted. "Look behind you!" It was no use. They continued to smile and wave at her, while the man in back of them got closer and closer. All of a sudden he reached into his coat. Penny was gasping for breath and hoarse from shouting. Why couldn't they hear her? The man was directly in back of them and was reaching out for her dad when Penny gave a final warning shout and woke up. She was drenched with sweat and freezing at the same time. The sun was starting to set, and the night air was extremely chilly in the gazebo.

She got up and started up the path back to the house. Still feeling the uneasiness due to the bad dream and cold to the bone, she shivered uncontrollably and her teeth began to chatter. It seemed like miles to the house, but she knew it was only a short way. Reaching the back door, she looked back into the wooded yard. Nothing was there. *I'm really beginning to spook myself,* she thought. *I've got to stop this.* Dismissing the dream, she stepped inside the back door.

"I was just going to send Ben out to get you," said her aunt. "He said you weren't wearing a coat, and it gets pretty chilly at night. My word, look at you; you're shaking. Ben!

Get a blanket. Come sit down here by the oven." Pushing Penny into a chair, Martha took the blanket Ben had retrieved from the closet and proceeded to wrap it around her.

"I should have warned you about the evenings. Oh, my! I hope you don't get sick," fretted her aunt as she pulled off Penny's damp shoes and dried her feet.

Penny sat up when her teeth finally stopped chattering and reassured her aunt that she was fine.

"I fell asleep and the time got away from me. I'm sorry for worrying you, Aunt Martha," said a remorseful Penny.

"It's okay. But if you're sure you're warm enough now, I want you to go upstairs and soak in a hot bath. When you get through, come on down to supper."

Penny dropped the blanket on the chair and went through the dining room to the foyer and up the stairs.

Relaxing in a hot tub of water, Penny thought about her dream; nightmare she thought, would be the more correct definition. She could not remember ever having nightmares. It was so strange. Before the dreams were always sort of blissful memories of happier times with her mom and dad. The transition into these horrible nightmares was really shaking her up. Was it a premonition, maybe? Who was the mysterious man she kept seeing?

She shook the thoughts away and started to bathe. Still feeling tired and sleepy, she thought she would beg off supper and go to bed early. Slipping on some shorts and a baggy shirt, she tied up her hair and went on down to the living room. Devin was standing with his back to her, watching TV. Not hearing her come in, he continued to watch what looked to her to be a game of soccer.

Penny backed out of the room, hoping to get back up the stairs before being seen. *What a mess I must look,* she thought. Just as she had retreated from the room, Martha spoke to her. "I see some color in your cheeks now. Do you feel any better?"

Penny wanted to crawl in a hole somewhere. She didn't mind her aunt seeing her looking such a mess, but she was mortified that Devin now would.

"I feel a lot better," she said, a lot more calmly than she felt. "The hot bath was just what I needed."

The two women's voices brought Devin into the foyer. "Martha tells me you feel under the weather. Maybe we should cancel the fishing trip until you're feeling better."

"Oh, no!" Penny fairly shouted, then catching herself added, "I'm just a little overwhelmed by everything that has happened the last few days. A good night's rest will fix me right up."

"Well, if you're sure, I'll see you in the morning." He gave them each a slight tip of his hat and went out the door.

Because of her appearance, she was half glad he wasn't staying, yet sorry he left. Penny was confused about her feelings toward him. Before she could pinpoint any tangible reason for her flip-flopping pulse, her aunt broke into her thoughts. "Are you ready for a light supper, dear?"

Forgetting her earlier desire to go on to bed, Penny nodded her head. She just wasn't ready to face the turmoil of her emotions alone.

"I made some chicken soup, my mom's cure-all remedy for what ails you," said Martha. "You looked so done in when you first came in. I hope you're not angry with me for calling Devin."

Penny smiled at her aunt's anxious expression and reassured her that she wasn't annoyed with her at all. As a matter of fact, she had to admit Aunt Martha's mothering was a welcome change. Lesley had always been like a mother to her, more so, she guessed, than her real mom; but Les wasn't real demonstrative, and it was rare when her true feelings came to the surface. Aunt Martha's fluttering around her like a mother hen was something she could get used to with no trouble at all.

Martha had the soup sitting in front of her in a second and the aroma made her mouth water. She could feel the warmth from her head to her toes as the hot liquid slowly made its way to her stomach.

"This is delicious!" exclaimed Penny between spoonfuls.

Martha beamed back a smile, happily accepting the compliment.

"I almost forgot to tell you. Kit and Kathleen will be over Saturday. I'll be baking and cooking most of the day tomorrow, so if you're sure you feel up to it, Devin's agreed to keep you company most of the day. As usual, they only gave me one day's notice, just like my Kit. Never stops to think we don't have children here much and that it may require a little bit of time to get goodies baked for them."

Penny listened while her aunt went on and on about how inconsiderate children were but saw through her cluckings to see just how excited she was to have the grandchildren over. "How long will they be staying?" she asked.

"Kit said maybe a whole week. He always says that though, and they usually stay only four or five days. However long it is, I can't wait."

Penny finished her soup then excused herself, noticing that her aunt was totally preoccupied with the next day's preparations for her family. Once upstairs, she slipped into the nightgown she had worn the previous night. Exhaustion overtook her as she slipped into bed and pulled up the spread. In just a few minutes she was fast asleep.

V

Waking up fully refreshed the next morning, Penny dressed in jeans and a long-sleeved shirt, which she wore over a sleeveless tank top. Grabbing a short jacket out of the closet, she left the room. As she pulled the door shut, she thought she heard a sound from the end of the hall. Straining her eyes, she looked down the corridor into the darkness. Nothing looked out of place, so she continued down the stairs, failing to see the silhouette of the man coming out of the room at the end of the hall. He followed her to the top of the stairs and watched her descent.

Feeling a prickling sensation at the base of her neck, Penny turned abruptly and looked back up the staircase, but the man at the top had retreated into the shadows. Feeling extremely stupid for her uneasiness, Penny continued into the dining room. She hadn't expected anyone to be up at this hour and was prepared to fix her own coffee in the kitchen. The surprise must have shown on her face as her aunt laughed at her expression and told her to come into the kitchen to have her coffee.

"Heard you coming down the stairs. Been up half the night myself; slept a couple of hours and got back up around four I guess it was."

Keeping up a steady conversation, her aunt continued working on what looked like enough baked delicacies for an army. Absently listening to her ramblings, Penny took in her aunt's appearance and could imagine what a beauty she must have been at her own age. Her cheeks were rosy with the heat from the oven. Her hair was damp with wisps curled all around her face. Eating a biscuit placed in front of her, along with the hot coffee, Penny was concentrating on her aunt's one-sided conversation, when she felt a tap on her shoulder. Turning around, she looked right into Devin's eyes. Speech eluded her and breathing was a little difficult.

Blaming her lack of oral response to fright, Devin hurriedly said, "Sorry to startle you. I thought you heard me come in." Satisfied that Penny was all right, he turned his attention to his aunt. "Got a cup of coffee for me, Martha?" he asked, as he lowered himself onto the stool next to Penny.

Martha put the hot mug of coffee, along with biscuits dripping with fresh butter, in front of him. Smiling his thanks, he devoured the biscuits and gulped down the coffee.

"Ready to go?" he asked, in what seemed like two seconds.

"Sure," replied Penny, finally finding her tongue.

She slipped off the stool and followed the departing Devin out of the house. Devin opened the door of the Jeep for Penny to get in. He could see by the surprised look on her face that she hadn't expected to go by car.

"Think we were taking the horses?" he asked.

"Well, yes, I suppose," she replied, somewhat disappointed.

"Where we're going is too far for a fishing trip by horseback. If you enjoy yourself today, maybe later on we can take a couple of day trips with the horses."

"Fine," said Penny.

Devin loaded the picnic lunch Martha had packed and got in back of the wheel. "It's about sixty miles from here, so settle back and enjoy the scenery."

Penny did just that. The sun was beginning to rise, putting a glow of newness to the surrounding countryside. Devin proved to be quite a charming host, pointing out the different flowers and plants along the way. The green and red flowers she admired on the way to her aunt's were called Kangaroo Paws. The orange-gold blooms were banksias. Devin's voice had a deep bass masculine intonation, which Penny found very much to her liking.

The trip to the lake was over much too soon. Devin unloaded all the fishing equipment and folding chairs from the Jeep. Penny got the bait bucket and picnic basket from the back and followed him to a beautiful spot under the trees. Looking across the lake, her eyes came upon a black majestic water bird. Devin motioned for her to be silent. Coming close he whispered that it was a black swan. It had to have been the most elegant bird she had ever seen. Something must have spooked it however, for it was taking off across the lake, wings outstretched and flapping. The lake itself was awesome. The sun glistened across its surface, casting shadowy outlines of the trees all around it.

Devin watched as the woman in front of him was held motionless by the strikingly beautiful display before them. He didn't quite know how to take her. She was childlike in the total joy she took from the beauty around them. She also reminded him a lot of Angela, although she looked absolutely nothing like her. Where Penny was fair-skinned; Angela had been olive. Penny had auburn hair; Angela's had been almost blue-black. Penny had brown eyes; Angela's had been, as he well remembered, the color of the sky. He had been totally and completely in love with Angela.

He was eight when she was born, and he had been a big brother to her through their childhood. This relationship had given them a strong bond with each other. The bond had grown into adolescent admiration and finally into adult love. They had just discovered the true feelings they held for one other when Angela had found out how sick she was. He would never forget their last meeting alone with each other. Devin had been expecting to finally be able to tell everyone they were in love and wanted to get married. He was destroyed when Angela, through tears, told him what the doctor had said. She told him that all the plans to tell everyone of their engagement would have to wait. He had begged her to let him go through the tests, treatment, and therapy, by her side. But she had remained steadfast in her decision in going it alone, stating she would not come to him an invalid. If the treatments cured her, they would tell everyone of their plans; but as it turned out, that never came to pass. He had watched at a distance as she withered away in such a short period of time to just a skeleton of the girl he loved. The last time he saw her, she barely knew he was there she was in so much pain. Martha had entered the room just in time to see him planting a kiss on her forehead. She had hugged him to her and told him that Angela had confessed her feelings for him the previous week. He and Martha did not leave Angela's side until she died later that evening.

After the funeral, heartbroken, Devin had gone back to the ranch and lost himself in his work. He hadn't thought about Angela and that time in his life for a while now, up until Penny arrived. It wasn't so much that there was any resemblance, but her childlike innocent outlook on life reminded him a lot of Angela. Even some of the clothes she was wearing brought back memories of some of the times he'd shared with her.

Returning to the present, Devin saw that Penny had unfolded her chair and was baiting her hook. "Here, let me do that for you," he offered.

"I've got to admit I don't particularly like this part of fishing, but I will bait my own hook if I have to," said Penny, with a crooked smile as she handed him her hook. Devin smiled back and threaded the worm on the barb. While he baited his and wiped his hands, Penny cast out her line into the lake.

"Good cast," he commented.

"Thanks. My dad and I fished together a lot. I really miss that, you know?"

He nodded, then cast his line into the water and sat down. They sat in companionable silence as the birds sang, frogs and crickets croaked, and the world woke up.

"Devin?" began Penny.

"Hmm?" replied Devin.

"I really appreciate your taking the time to make my stay here more enjoyable—"

Devin held up his hand and broke in. "Don't mention it at all. I sort of needed some vacation time myself, and we're doing what I'd be doing if I was by myself. So you see, it's no sacrifice on my part at all. In fact, just to make you feel like you're not taking advantage of my good nature, I'll let you clean the fish. How's that?" he asked with a big grin.

Penny broke down and laughed. "I don't feel that guilty," she said, wrinkling up her nose.

The ice broken, they both started talking more freely to each other, exchanging, as the day wore on, more about each other than any other person close to them would ever know.

After eating the delicious fried chicken, potato salad, and sliced pound cake, they both lay back on the blanket, completely enjoying the peace and quiet. Comfortable and at ease with Devin, Penny drifted off to sleep.

Devin had been watching her eyes slowly closing. He smiled to himself when he realized the trust she seemed to have in him. Propping himself up on one elbow, he watched as she slept. Her hair had blown across her cheek, making her quite a pretty picture lying there. Starting to feel a little uncomfortable at his thoughts and reactions to her, he lay back down and looked up at the sky.

Dan had come to him last week and told him Les and Penny were coming over for what Penny thought was a get-away-vacation type of trip. Since Zack's death, Dan had been very agitated and secretive around him. The day of their arrival, he had pulled Devin aside and confided in him that the sheep deaths and Zack's apparent stroke, he thought, were somehow connected with each other. He said he couldn't go into detail, but he was afraid Penny would some-how now be in danger. It was all confusing to Devin, but he loved and trusted Dan and followed his instructions to the letter.

Dan had adopted him when his mother and dad had run off and left him twenty years ago. He'd never heard anything more from them and, as far as he knew, neither had his grandmother, Myree. She had been prepared to raise him herself, but Dan, having never been married and not expecting to, was glad to have a son follow in his footsteps. Devin had been so proud to have someone who really wanted him and treated him no different than a real son. He would do anything for Dan, so here he was, playing nursemaid and bodyguard to Penny. *Not such a bad job at that,* he thought to himself.

Penny stirred, opened her eyes, and looked around. Re-alizing what she had done, she blushed beet red and sat up. "I'm so sorry," she stuttered.

"Not to worry. Just woke up myself," he lied. "Guess we're like a couple of pigs; eat, then sleep." They both laughed at that and stood up.

"We'd better be getting back. It'll be dark before long."

Penny folded up the blanket and repacked the basket, while Devin loaded all the fishing equipment and threw back the two fish they had caught.

"It's a good thing we don't have to eat what we caught for supper," said Penny, laughing.

"Yeah, I guess so," agreed Devin, as they both got in the Jeep and started back to the house.

Penny felt contented after the day's events. She felt she knew Devin a little better and liked what she had learned. Finding out he was adopted made her feel a little better about the not-so-cousinly way she had begun to think of him. He seemed to enjoy being with her too and did a lot for her small ego.

The ride back was in comfortable silence and much too short. Devin stopped in front of the house to let her out. Waving aside his offer to help her in with the blanket and basket, she bounded up the steps.

Inside, everyone was aflutter. Ben was motioning for her to follow him. Dropping the basket and blanket on the floor, she followed him to a room beyond the staircase that she hadn't noticed before. Lying in a huge four-poster bed, her aunt looked like she was dead. Running to the side of the bed, Penny knelt beside her and shook her slightly. Martha's eyes popped open and she smiled up at her.

"Sorry to scare you, dear, but I guess I sort of overdid it in the kitchen. The heat must have gotten to me; anyway, there's plenty of supper prepared for you—"

Penny hushed her aunt up and said, "Don't you worry about me. Just rest. Is there anything I can do for you? Do we need to get Uncle Ned?"

"Lord no, child! This has happened before. I keep forgetting, don't ask me how, that I'm not as young and slim as I used to be. I was working away and the next thing I knew Ben and the staff had me in here. I don't know what I'd do without him."

As if summoned, Ben reappeared with a tray of tea and sandwiches. Propping her aunt up with pillows, he placed the tray in front of her. Penny fixed her tea and sat beside her as she sipped the strong brew.

"Go on out now. Don't worry about me. By morning I'll be fine. One thing though, if you don't mind, please ask Devin if he'll stay in the guest room. He knows which one it is. I'll feel better knowing he's inside."

Penny nodded and looked at Ben. He took the tray and left the room. Helping her aunt lie down again, she gave Martha a kiss, then tiptoed out when she had gone back to sleep. Penny was on her way to ask Ben where to find Devin when he came flying in the door.

"Is she all right?" he asked.

"Yes," Penny reassured him. "She's gone to sleep now, but she asked if you would stay here tonight."

"Sure, no problem," replied Devin, as he sat down in the chair in back of him. Penny then realized how scared he had been when he first came in. His face was ashen.

"Devin, please don't worry. She cooked all day in the hot kitchen for Kit and Kathleen and really overdid it. She says she'll be okay in the morning."

Devin nodded and stood up. "I'll go get my things. Be right back," he said and went out the door.

Penny went into the dining room to find Ben. He was by the table. He had a pad of paper in front of him and was writing something on it. In just a minute he handed it over to her. Funny, this somehow had never occurred to her. *Of course he can write, you idiot,* she chided herself. The hastily scribbled note said that he would be staying inside the main house tonight also. If she needed anything, just get him in the room off of the kitchen.

Penny nodded, then told him she would be spending the night on the chaise she saw in her aunt's room.

"I'll feel much better near her if she needs me," she explained. For the first time since she arrived, Ben smiled at Penny and left the room.

Very much aware that Devin would be back in a short time, Penny bounded up the stairs to her bedroom. She undressed in record time, showered, and changed into a nightgown and robe. Slipping her feet into soft slippers, the only ones that would fit her, she started back down the stairs to her aunt's room. Devin had started up the stairs and they met each other halfway.

"Ben says you're staying in Martha's room," said Devin as he slowly took in her fresh, wholesome appearance. Feeling light-headed this close to him, Penny managed to softly answer, "Yes."

"If she gets worse, God forbid, come and get me. I'll be in the room next to yours."

Penny nodded once again and hurried the rest of the way down the steps. Devin watched her descent and continued to watch her until she reached her aunt's room. Damn! She had an overpowering effect on him. *I'll have to watch my step with her,* he thought, then turned around and continued up to the guest room.

Penny had inched open the door to her aunt's room and entered, not wanting to disrupt her sleep. She could hear her slow, even breathing. The lamp in the corner cast a shadow across the figure on the bed. Tiptoeing over, Penny checked her color and felt her head. Everything seemed to be in order, so she lay back on the chaise and pulled up the blanket at the bottom. She thought back over the day's events and flushed with warmth at her visions of Devin. *I've got to get a hold of myself,* she thought. *I'm just a job, a J-O-B, he has to carry out, an assignment, chore,* she chided herself. Determined to put all thoughts of him out of her mind, she closed her eyes and willed herself to sleep.

VI

Devin was having much more difficulty handling the situation than Penny. He hadn't been upstairs since Angela's death and it brought memories of her back to him in full force. Slipping into her room, he slowly took in the bed, which now had Angela's clothes that Penny had been wearing lying where she had thrown them. The scent that filled his nostrils was of Penny, along with the light fragrance of freshness that seemed to follow her everywhere. He tried to picture Angela in his mind, but the image of Penny on the blanket sleeping this afternoon filled his thoughts.

This is crazy, he thought as he left the room and reentered his own. Lying across the bed and closing his eyes, he drifted off to sleep.

Awakening abruptly, Devin listened, while letting his eyes adjust to the darkness of the room. Something had woken him up, but what? He wondered. It sounded like a drawer opening up, but where? Straining his ears, he tried to focus all his senses on the slight noise. Penny's room! He was sure that's where the sound was coming from.

Slowly easing himself off the bed, he grabbed his revolver from his duffle and quietly opened the door. Looking out into the darkness of the hallway, he peered first left, then right. Seeing nothing he slipped to Penny's door. Slowly he turned the knob. Pushing into the room in a rush, while at the same time flipping on the light, Devin looked all around. Everything seemed to be as he had left it hours earlier. He looked in the bathroom and into the closet. Nothing. Feeling foolish, he started back out the door. Then he noticed it. The window was halfway open. Going across the room in a couple of strides, Devin peered out. Total darkness was all he could see. He closed the window and fastened the lock on top. As he turned around, his eyes caught a glimpse of something moving under the bed. Carefully stepping to the opposite wall, he crouched down on his heels and looked under the bed.

It was a snake! *What the hell!* he thought, then moved with great efficiency and speed. Knowing if he used the gun he would wake up the whole house, he resorted to catching the snake alive It was almost to the other side of the bed. Getting on top of the bed, he crawled over to the far side. He grabbed it right in back of its head as it crawled from under the bed. It had to be at least three and a half to four feet long. Keeping a good hold on its head, he picked up the body and carried the snake down the stairs. Going through the kitchen, Devin grabbed the big butcher knife on the cutting board and made short work of the nonvenomous reptile. Throwing the pieces of the snake out in the garbage, he turned around and faced Ben, who had a machete held high.

"Whoa! It's me, Ben!" yelled Devin, as he held up his hands to ward off the blow. Ben lowered the long blade and with a thankful sigh then sank into the closest chair.

Devin knew an explanation was in order, so he proceeded to disclose to Ben what had happened. He had no idea who would put a nonpoisonous snake in the room and for that matter why. All he could come up with was that someone was trying to scare the hell out of Penny. He could tell this information upset the small man a lot. So with heads bent and pen and paper ready, the two men talked and planned until the sun came up.

VII

Penny woke to the sound of excited voices. Easing up from the chaise, she saw her aunt surrounded by people unfamiliar to her. The man was a lot taller than Martha, while the woman standing next to him was very short. The two children were jumping up and down, each one trying to get their grandmother's undivided attention. Penny slipped off the chaise and out of the room unnoticed. Rushing up the stairs before someone saw her in such a disheveled state, she nearly collided with Devin.

"I'm sorry," she whispered, trying to catch her breath.

"Is the house on fire or something?" he asked, a smile touching the corners of his mouth.

"No, nothing like that," Penny answered, excusing herself as she slid into her bedroom and shut the door.

At least Aunt Martha looks totally recovered from yesterday's illness, she thought, smiling to herself as she remembered the expression of pure joy on her aunt's face. Humming, she quickly dressed, brushed her hair, and applied a dab of lipstick. Very much wanting to make a good impression on her cousins, she checked her reflection one more time before heading downstairs.

Laughter was coming from the dining room as she entered. Aunt Martha was flushed and laughing like a child.

"Come in, Penny. Meet Kit and Kathy," said her aunt.

Penny went around the table toward the couple and held out her hand. Kathy stood up and embraced her and

Kit followed suit. Penny felt a little odd but, not wanting to seem unfriendly, hugged them back.

Kit was a mixture of both parents. Tall, lean, and muscular like his dad but with light hair and a complexion like his mom. Kathy was beautiful. She had dark coal black hair, the greenest eyes Penny had ever seen, a knockout figure, and was very small and petite. Penny guessed she couldn't be any more than five feet tall, if that. She was totally taken in by her natural beauty. The kids were one of each. The boy looked like his mom and was probably around three or four years old. The girl was the image of her dad and just toddling around, holding on to everyone as she went. She was adorable. Penny reached down and picked her up. Aunt Martha smiled at Penny and started filling in the gaps for her about the children.

"Mandy there is ten months old. Isn't she a beauty?" said the proud grandmother, beaming. Not waiting for an answer, she continued. "Jess is four and a half and just like his dad in every action and deed. They're a fine pair, don't you think?"

Laughing at Mandy, who was trying to pull the ribbon out of her hair, Penny had to agree. She had never been around children before, so this was quite a delightful experience. Jess took off running for the hallway as Devin entered the room.

"Uncle Dev!" he yelled.

Devin reached down and swung the excited boy up in the air.

"You must have grown a foot, young man," he teased.

Jess giggled as Devin tossed him up in the air time after time. Mandy was squirming in Penny's arms, trying to get down.

"Here, give her to me," said Kathy, as she lifted the baby from Penny. Devin stopped tossing Jess and carried him on into the room.

"Kit, Kathy, good to see you both again," he said, holding out his one free hand.

"Damn, Dev," said Kit, catching Devin's hand in a strong shake, "you're as dark as Ben. Uncle Dan keeping you in the saddle year round now?"

Devin laughed, gave Jess to his dad, and gave Kathy a hug. "I see you're still putting up with this overgrown kid."

Kathy smiled at both men, enjoying the playful banter between them.

After a lengthy catchup conversation, the group looked up as Martha reentered the room, cheeks flushed rosy red and smiling.

"Well, Mom, we're starved," stated Kit, as everyone took a seat and looked with anticipation to their hostess. Martha went out into the kitchen and along with Ben, started bringing plate after plate of steaming sausages, bacon, biscuits, pancakes, and more. Everyone dug into the food like they hadn't eaten in months. Even the children did justice to the feast set before them. Martha continued fussing around everyone until they all sat back, totally stuffed and miserable.

"Good grief," cried Kathy. "I've just put on ten pounds; I know it," she said, as she rubbed her stomach as if in pain.

Martha looked happily around at everyone. "I'm so glad you all are here," she said, with tears glistening in her eyes.

"Aw, come on now," said Kit, pushing away from the table and going over to his mother, "none of this teary, gushy stuff, okay."

Martha pushed him away and laughed. "Let's go on into the living room and let them clean up in here. Come, Jess," she said, leading her small grandson by the hand into the other room.

For the next several days, Penny totally forgot all her past troubles and sadness. Mandy and Jess had captured her heart and filled her days.

Mornings were spent helping Kathy bathe and dress both children. Then came the long walks, playing tag with Jess and patty-cake with Mandy. She and Kathy hit it off immediately, and Kit self-appointed himself as her big brother. Aunt Martha was in her glory as doting mother, aunt, and grandmother, and Penny got to see Devin in his role as uncle to the two children. When Kit told his mom they would have to be leaving the next day, Penny couldn't believe that a week had passed and it was Thursday already.

"Where did the time go?" she asked her aunt.

"Honey, every time the kids come, I ask myself the same question. I tried to get Kit to stay longer, but they have to get back to work. Ned will be sorry to have missed them. I was hoping they would stay until he got back. Oh well, let me go scare up supper."

As her aunt retreated, Penny went in search of Kathy and the kids. She found Kathy in the gazebo in back of the house.

"Penny," said Kathy, "this has been one of the most enjoyable visits I've had in a very long time. I really hate to leave tomorrow and wouldn't, if it weren't for Kit's job."

Kathy was filling up with tears, which made Penny also misty eyed. The two young women hugged each other.

"Do you think before you go back home you would like to come into Sydney and stay with us for a couple of days or so?" asked Kathy.

"Sure," agreed Penny, feeling happy that Kathy felt the same way as she did about her. "This has been a wonderful week for me also. I feel like I've known you all my life, and I just love the kids. I'm going to miss you all so much," said Penny, blinking rapidly.

Just then Kit came up and, seeing how upset both women were, asked, "Is something wrong?"

"No, silly," said Kathy as she linked her arm through his. "It's just that neither one of us had a sister or a real close friend. Now we know what we've missed all these years."

"Well, it's not the end of the world, you know," said Kit, in his sweet gentle manner. "You know you can come with us, Penny, and stay as long as you like."

Kathy was nodding her head up and down and smiling from ear to ear. "Oh, please, Penny, come home with us," she begged.

As much as Penny would have liked to have done just that, she knew she needed to stay with her aunt until Les and her uncles returned. No one had mentioned Martha's collapse to Kit and Kathy, and Penny didn't want to leave her here all alone.

"As soon as Les gets back, I promise I'll come for a few days, okay?" replied Penny.

Kathy nodded. "I guess that will have to do."

With that decision out of the way, the threesome returned to the house.

The next morning Penny rose early and went downstairs to help Aunt Martha with breakfast. Jess was sitting in the kitchen, jelly smeared all over the bottom half of his face. Smiling broadly, he offered some of his dripping biscuit to Penny.

"No, thanks," she said, grabbing a cloth and dabbing at the sticky goo on his chin.

Kathy came into the kitchen with Mandy, a worried look on her face. "Mom, Mandy's real warm and her stomach has been running off this morning."

Martha took the listless baby from Kathy. "She's burning up!" said Martha, as she felt Mandy's forehead. "Have you given her anything for this fever yet?"

"Yes, of course, Mom," Kathy reassured her. "She's had three doses since about one o'clock though, and the fever isn't coming down." Kit came in just in time to hear the exchange between his wife and mother.

"Mom, we're leaving right now. We should get into Sydney just in time to catch Dr. Franklin before he leaves for the weekend. I've already called and let them know we were coming."

Martha nodded her head and kissed everyone good-bye. "Call me as soon as you see the doctor. Don't forget now!" she yelled as they drove away.

Penny put her arm around her aunt's shoulders. "Don't worry now, Aunt Martha," she said, trying to reassure herself as well. "She's just getting a cold or a twenty-four-hour virus or something like that."

"You're probably right, child," agreed her aunt. "I can't help but worry though; she was fine last night."

Penny followed her aunt back inside and into the kitchen.

"You hungry?" asked Martha.

"No, not really. A cup of tea sounds good though."

The two women fixed tea and, sipping on the hot brew, gazed into space, each lost in her own thoughts.

Waiting for Kit's call was making a nervous wreck out of both women. Martha would stare at the phone as if her will alone could make it ring. At five o'clock, unable to restrain herself any longer, Martha dialed her son's house. Getting the answering machine, she left a message for him to call. When an hour had passed and there was still no call, Penny thought she would have to put her aunt into restraints. Pacing back and forth, Martha kept up a constant one-sided conversation.

"He knows what a worry wart I am. I just don't understand his not calling by now. Something's wrong; something is bad wrong," she kept saying over and over again.

Penny really felt her aunt was overreacting, but she kept trying to soothe her. "I'm sure she's okay. It was probably just a virus or the flu and they've gone to the store after the doctor's visit. Kit will call any time now; you'll see. Everything will be just fine, and you will be kicking yourself for getting so worked up."

"You're probably right, Pen, but I've got this feeling. I sure hope I'm wrong."

Trying to take her aunt's mind off of Mandy, Penny asked if she wanted to play a game of rummy.

"No, dear, I appreciate what you're trying to do, but I just couldn't concentrate."

Just then the phone rang. Martha answered it before the first ring was completed.

"Yes, Kit, what did he say?"

Penny could only guess what Kit was saying, but realized it wasn't good news when she saw her Aunt Blanche.

"Here, Penny, Kit wants to say something to you," said her aunt, handing the phone to her.

"Hello, Kit," said Penny.

"Listen carefully, Pen. I just told Mom they're keeping Mandy for observation tonight at Saint Matthews Hospital. She wants to come now, but I want her to wait till the tests come back tomorrow."

"What do they think is wrong?" asked Penny, now completely shaken.

"The doctor thinks it's some kind of bacterial virus. Mandy's lost a lot of fluids and they've got an IV in her. The fever is still high. I just don't know what to think, Pen. Kathy is about to come unglued, and the one thing she doesn't need tonight is Mom going to pieces on her too."

Penny could hear the exhaustion in Kit's voice. "Tell Kathy we love her and will pray for Mandy. I'll try to calm

Aunt Martha, but I can't guarantee it will work. When will you call us with the test results?"

"Dr. Franklin said we will have them first thing in the morning. I'll call right away. If it is anything bad, I'll certainly want Mom here. In the meantime, she needs to get some rest in case we do need her to come."

Penny took down the room and phone number of the hospital before Kit hung up. Aunt Martha was sitting in the recliner in a daze. Penny knelt down in front of her and gave her a hug. "Kit wants you to get some rest in case you need to go there tomorrow. They'll need you to relieve them, so you need to be refreshed."

Her aunt looked at her and nodded her head in agreement. Then all of a sudden, she snapped out of the daze she was in. "Look at me acting like the child had died, for heaven's sake. Kit's right.. I need to get a good night's sleep or I won't be any good to them at all. Penny, you need to rest too. If I have to go, you'll have to drive me there. Devin left this morning for the camp and won't be back until tomorrow night. He wasn't expecting Kit and Kathy to leave until tomorrow. Come on now, let's go on to bed."

Penny kissed her aunt good night at the door to her bedroom and continued on up to her own room. She didn't have the heart to tell her aunt that she didn't have a driver's license. She knew how to drive all right, having driven her dad's car around the land and to the minute market close to the house. It just wasn't a necessity for her to get her license. *No need to worry about that now,* she told herself, as she undressed and slipped into the tub.

Feeling much better and relaxed after the bath, Penny slipped under the covers. She said a prayer for Mandy like she promised she would and brushed back the tears slipping from under her lashes.

"Oh, God, please let that little baby shrug off whatever it is that is ailing her. We all love her so much."

Penny hadn't realized how upset she really was. Crying softly, she drifted off to sleep.

Penny's dreams were full of her mom that night. Off and on till the wee hours of dawn, she tossed and turned, trying to still the haunted images of her in the last days of her life. Waking fully, Penny got out of bed and put on the robe that was lying across the chair. She slipped down the stairs and headed for the kitchen, trying to find her way in the dark without disturbing anyone's sleep.

As she neared the kitchen door, she noticed light coming from the bottom. *That's strange,* she thought. *Maybe Ben's up.* So without another thought, she opened the door. The light had been turned off and the room was in total darkness. Feeling for the switch on the wall, Penny inched her way into the room. Finally finding it, she flipped on the light. Fear engulfed her. She knew without a doubt someone had turned out the light as soon as she touched the door. Seeing no one, she went over to the back door. It was closed but not locked. *That's not like Ben,* she thought, remembering the nightly ritual Ben and her aunt had of checking the locks before going to bed. Penny checked every corner and cranny in the room. She even checked the broom closet, half expecting someone to jump out at her. *I'll have to ask Ben about the door,* she told herself as she fixed a glass of warm milk. Swallowing the last drops of liquid, Penny washed out her glass and went back upstairs. The milk did its trick and helped her to sleep, this time dreamlessly.

VIII

Ben was shaking her awake and motioning for her to hurry and get dressed. Penny jumped out of bed and dressed in record time. Aunt Martha was carrying an overnight bag out the front door as she came into the hallway.

"Hurry and pack enough for a couple of days," she told Penny. "Kit called. Mandy's in a coma."

Penny's heart dropped to her feet. Turning around, she ran back upstairs and threw several things into the canvas bag she found in the closet. Meeting her aunt at the car, Ben took her bag and put it in the trunk. Martha gave her the keys and they both jumped into the front seat. Penny wasn't even nervous about driving; there was no time for it. Starting the car, she looked at her aunt expectantly.

"Just follow the dirt road out to the pavement," she said. "I'll tell you which way to go as we get to the turns."

"What exactly did Kit say?" asked Penny as they drove off.

"The fever won't break. They're pumping antibiotics intravenously into her, but nothing's happening. She went into a coma about five o'clock this morning. They moved her into pediatric ICU. That's all he could get out before he broke down. I told him we'd be there as fast as this car could go."

Penny took her eyes off the road long enough to glance over at her aunt. She had to admire the way she was holding up.

"I see you looking at me, Pen. Don't worry. I do great in an emergency. Always have. I only fall apart when it's all over."

"How far is Sydney?" Penny asked.

"Three hundred and forty-two miles," replied her aunt. "We'd take a plane, but the closest airport is outside of Sydney. Just drive carefully but fast, okay?"

Penny nodded and from that point on, concentrated on the road before her. They were three hours into the trip when her aunt asked her to stop and gas up. Glancing at the gas gauge, Penny realized they were almost on empty. She pulled into the next station, drove to the pumps, and cut the engine. Aunt Martha got out and went into the restroom.

Penny hadn't realized how tightly she had been gripping the steering wheel and had to practically peel her fingers from around it. After massaging her hand she opened the door. A young boy, maybe eight or nine years old at the most, was pumping her gas. Smiling at him, she went on into the small grocery store that was part of the service station.

A wonderful smell met her nostrils as she opened the door. It was then that she realized they hadn't eaten anything since Kit and Kathy had left yesterday. Knowing they needed nourishment to keep up their strength, she bought some sandwiches and drinks for the rest of their journey. Getting back in the car, she handed her aunt the bag.

"How stupid of me!" exclaimed her aunt. "I was so upset this morning, I never thought about food. I bet this is a first for me!"

Penny and Martha looked at each other and burst out laughing. That seemed to relieve some of the tension.

Penny drove out of the station, while Aunt Martha handed her a sandwich. "You want to stop to eat?" she asked. Penny shook her head no and they continued on their way.

Reaching Sydney at noon was a mistake. The traffic was horrible, which made Penny all the more nervous. Thank goodness Aunt Martha knew her way around well enough to direct her straight to the hospital with no problem. They met Kit outside of the ICU unit.

"I came out about fifteen minutes ago," he said. "I figured you would be getting here about now. Mom, Kathy is exhausted, but I can't get her to come leave Mandy. Please go in there and see if she'll let you stay."

Martha put on the face mask needed to go into the unit. After wrapping two gowns around her, she went inside. It seemed like hours before she came back out.

"Penny," she said, removing her mask, "I can't do anything with the child. See if you can get her to leave. She's about to drop."

Penny knew from talking to Kit that there had been no change in Mandy's condition. She entered the room and was shocked when she saw Kathy. It looked like she had aged ten years in the last two days. She didn't seem to be aware that anyone had entered the room until Penny went over and hugged the worn-out girl.

"Penny," she sobbed, grabbing her tightly, "she won't wake up. I talk to her and sing to her. I've rubbed her back until you can see my hand print on it. Oh, what if she never comes to?" sobbed the young mother, now totally out of control.

Penny couldn't do anything but hold Kathy and try to calm her. "Look, Kathy," she said, "Aunt Martha came to relieve you for a while. You're not going to do Mandy any good if you get sick yourself. Just take a long enough break to shower and get something to eat. I'll stay with Aunt Martha and Mandy. We'll call you if anything changes before you get back."

Kathy looked up at Penny and saw the concern and love in her eyes. "Okay, Pen, but you'll call . . ." she started, and Penny nodded her head.

Kathy leaned over the sleeping baby and kissed her gently on the cheek. She looked just like she was taking a nap. It was hard to believe she was so ill.

When Kathy left, Penny went over to Mandy and felt her forehead. She was still extremely hot and looked pitiful with the IV coming out of her arm. Penny started filling up with tears, but chastised herself. *You've got to be strong for Kathy and Kit,* she told herself. Just then Aunt Martha came into the room.

"Kit's taking Kathy home for a while. Thanks, Penny," said her aunt, patting her arm.

Sitting in the two chairs along the wall, Penny and Martha watched over the sleeping infant.

There was no noticeable change all that day and into the following afternoon. Kathy returned to the hospital rested and seemed to be in much better spirits. Kit, however, looked like the walking dead, but he was determined not to break down.

Kit had just taken Kathy and his mom down to the cafeteria to get some lunch. Penny was straightening the blanket around Mandy for the umpteenth time, when she noticed her little fingers wriggling. Calling the nurse, she kept watching the child's hands. She looked up at her face just as Mandy opened her eyes. Penny was ecstatic.

The nurse rushed into the room in a matter of seconds and tried to get her to leave for a few minutes while they checked Mandy over. Penny refused to leave. The nurse wasn't going to argue with her as Mandy was fully awake now and had started to yell very loudly.

The nurse had picked Mandy up and was trying to calm the baby down but was having no luck. Penny stepped forward and she handed the child to her. Mandy immediately stopped crying and wound her arms around Penny's neck.

The IV tube was twisted around the baby's wriggling body. Penny gently untangled the tubing the best she could. Thank God all the movement hadn't pulled it out of her little arm.

Kit, Kathy, and Martha entered the room at a run. As soon as she saw her mother, the wide-eyed Mandy started crying once more. Kathy took the child from Penny, hugging her until the little girl squirmed to be free.

Kit stood to the side, observing mother and child with a smile as big as the sun.

Aunt Martha sat down in the chair as if all of a sudden her legs wouldn't support her. Penny just stood back and took in the happy scene.

Dr. Franklin came into the room, followed by the harried nurse.

"I see Sleeping Beauty woke up," he said, as he listened to her heartbeat with his stethoscope.

Mandy's curiosity got the best of her, and she reached out for the end of the instrument. Letting her play, the doctor proceeded to disclose the latest results of the tests taken the previous day.

"There is definitely a foreign body, which none of our tests have been able to identify, in her blood samples. Not knowing what it is has made it quite difficult to treat. It seems like we hit the right combination though, looking at her now."

Mandy smiled up at the doctor and reached for his glasses. "Not so fast, young lady," he laughed, as he backed out of her reach and continued. "Yesterday's test results show a large decline in this strange chemical, due no doubt to the IV liquids being pumped into her so rapidly. We're going to need to keep her here until all trace of this substance is gone. Hopefully, by the time she's released, we will be able to pinpoint it." Looking around at the entire family and satisfied he had their undivided attention, he then asked, "Is there anything different she may have eaten or had to drink in the last week or two?" Talking back and forth with each other, they concluded that none of them could think of anything Mandy had ingested other than her formula and, of course, the food that they had also eaten.

"If you think of anything later on, let me know immediately," said the doctor as he left the room.

Aunt Martha was extremely upset at the implication that something she had fed her granddaughter could have caused this awful illness. Kit, completely exhausted and short-tempered, snapped at her. "Mom, please get control of yourself. *No one* has accused *you* of anything. All of us ate the same food and drank the same liquids, except, of course, the formula. Evidently the doctors are grabbing at straws here."

Martha taken aback at her son's curt tone, burst into tears. "That does it!" exploded Kit as he stomped out of the room.

Kathy looked at Martha then toward the door at her departing husband.

"Mom, please forgive Kit. He's tired and upset. Heck, we all are. Penny, could you please hold Mandy a minute?" asked Kathy, pushing the child into her arms. She then bent down, gave Martha a hug, and quickly left the room.

Mandy started crying, evidently upset at the earlier outburst and her grandmother's tears.

"Here, give her to me," said Martha, holding out her arms for the baby.

Penny handed Mandy over to her and sat in the only other chair in the room. The events of the last few minutes had left her quite shaken. Looking over at Aunt Martha, she noticed that she looked a lot more composed than a few minutes before. Mandy had stopped her whimpering and had drifted off to sleep. Aunt Martha motioned for Penny to put her back in the crib. Penny hurried over, took the sleeping infant from her aunt, and put her gently on the mattress. She looked just like an angel, her little mouth puckering and smiling.

Aunt Martha whispered that she was going to find some coffee and asked if she wanted anything. Penny shook her head and sat down in the chair vacated by her aunt so she could keep a closer eye on the sleeping child.

Mandy continued to improve with each day. Finally, the doctors agreed to release her from the hospital. Dr. Franklin cautioned them all to be very careful and watch closely for any recurring symptoms of the illness.

Kit and Martha had talked to each other right after his outburst and everything was forgiven. Penny was now extremely anxious to get back to her aunt and uncle's house. It had been a whole month now since Les, Ned, and Dan had left for the outback; and except for phone conversations with Aunt Les and her uncles about Mandy, they had not had time to really talk to one another. Penny had to admit she was really getting homesick for Aunt Les.

Aunt Martha was reluctant to leave her children and grandchildren, but she too was ready to return home. She and Penny got into the car with a lot more items than they'd originally brought. (Penny had gone shopping with Kathy to buy much-needed shoes and underthings for herself). Good-byes finally over, Penny and her aunt pulled out into traffic and started the long trip back.

IX

Les, Ned, and Dan reached camp around noon. Kurt and the others had the tents and gear all stowed. The lab equipment had been set up in a separate shelter. On the trip out to the camp, it was made very apparent to the trio just how serious the current situation was. They had passed several more dead sheep along the way and had biopsied some of the tissue. They stopped long enough to get a bite to eat, then immediately set to the task before them.

After their work collecting samples of dirt, grass, leaves, and water in the area around them, the tests displayed the usual results, except for the same foreign chemical that kept showing up. The characteristics and composition of this complex chemical were familiar to Les, although she couldn't put a name to it or find it in any of the textbooks. This was really beginning to bother her.

Les remembered her first conversation with Ned over the phone a couple of months ago. She couldn't believe then that he and Dan were convinced that Polly's, Angela's, and the sheeps' deaths were somehow related. Her feelings had changed, however, after Ned started giving her the results of the tests he had done up to that point. They had conversed after that first call on a pay phone to keep Penny, or anyone else for that matter, from overhearing the conversations. Les had been persuaded to come back to Australia and use her expertise in chemistry to help them solve the mystery.

After her arrival and seeing firsthand the slow destruction of the sheep, she realized her experience in this field was extremely important. Days merged into a week, which turned into a month. The three siblings were unaware of the passage of time, so caught up were they in unraveling the mystery of this chemical.

When Devin arrived, bringing news of Mandy's illness, Ned became very concerned. They all threw a few necessary items into bags and arrived home to find Penny and Martha had already left. Ned telephoned the hospital and talked to Martha. Mandy by then was doing fine and was going to be released that very day. Les and Dan were surprised to hear the change in Ned's tone the very next minute.

"They found what?" he shouted. "What do you mean they don't have a clue? What kind of quacks are treating her? Okay, okay, take your time and visit. We'll see you both when you get here. I love you too."

Ned looked at Les and Dan with deep concern on his face. "We have to retest the water in the well. I just checked it again a couple of months ago, but apparently something here caused my grandchild to nearly die."

Over the next few hours samples were collected and the tests conducted. The next day the results were positive. The same chemical was now in the well.

"We can't wait for Martha to get back," said Dan, calling Devin into the lab. "Son, the test results are positive. We have to leave right away for camp. Stay and look after Martha and Penny. We should be back within a week, or we'll send word."

Devin assured them all that he would take care of everything.

"Please tell Penny I'll send for her if we are going to be much longer," said Les.

Devin agreed to relay all the messages. Within an hour the three were packed and on their way.

X

Aunt Martha slept most of the way home, which showed Penny how much this trip had taken out of her. Reaching home around five P.M., Penny and Martha were greeted at the car by a smiling Ben. Leaving her aunt in his care, Penny bounded up the steps to the porch and into the house. Looking in both the dining room and living room for Aunt Les, she turned in the direction of Devin's voice as he walked out of the kitchen.

"Welcome home," he greeted her with a big smile and hug, which she readily returned.

"Where's Aunt Les?" she inquired.

"The lab results came back in last night. They left again this morning to do more testing. Les knew you would be disappointed, but she had me promise to reassure you that they would be back home in less than a week. If it's going to take longer, I'm to take you out to visit them at the camp. By the way, *no one* is to drink the well water or use it for anything other than bathing and flushing, understand?" Penny had been staring at Devin while he was talking. It hit her how much she had missed him. Pulling her hands from his and looking down, she tried to hide her feelings from his eyes. He was struggling with his own reaction to her return, however, and wasn't going to let her get off so easily. Pulling her chin up with his hand, he once again looked deep into her eyes. "I missed you," was all he got out before Ben and Aunt Martha came walking through the door.

Guiltily jumping back from each other as if caught in some wrongdoing, Penny hastened down the hallway and up the stairs to her room. She was trying to calm her wildly beating heart and rationalize what had just taken place. A knock at her door disturbed her thoughts.

"Yes?" she inquired as the door opened.

Megan entered, talking a mile a minute. "Guess this is a surprise for you! Dan wanted me here to help you and give you someone your own age to keep you company. I hope it's okay with you. If not, I'll be glad to go back home and—

"Hold it, hold it," Penny broke in, laughing. "I'm very happy to have you here. Aunt Martha is a dear, but it will be fun to have you to talk to."

Megan lit up like a light. "Great! I took the liberty of bringing up your bags. I'll just go get them from the hall."

Megan turned and went out the door. Picking up the numerous bags, she reentered the bedroom and walked over to the bed. Penny started to help her unpack the clothes, but Megan shooed her away and pushed her into the rocking chair. She then continued on with her chore.

Rather bushed from the trip and thinking back on her meeting with Devin, Penny decided to let the young woman complete her task. She was not accustomed to having someone wait on her. She didn't want to hurt Megan's feelings, but she would take this arrangement up with Aunt Martha in the morning. She had to admit, though, that having Megan around would break up the monotony until Aunt Les returned. It would also free up some of her time to analyze her feelings for Devin.

Getting out of the rocker, Penny went on into the bathroom and started to run her bath water. Megan was beside her in a minute. "I'll do that," she began, but Penny decided to draw the line right there.

"I think I'm more than capable of bathing myself, Megan. Go ahead with what you were doing, and I'll be out when I finish."

"Okay," said Megan, shrugging her shoulders as she left the bathroom. "You're the boss," Penny heard her mumble before the door closed.

I hope I didn't hurt her feelings, she thought, but cleared her mind of everything as she slipped into the tub. The steaming water warmed her body and soaked into her tired muscles. Stretching out to her full length, Penny relaxed and closed her eyes.

A picture of Devin came to her mind, and Penny tried to sort out her feelings for him. She hadn't realized how much she had missed him until seeing him downstairs. She felt a tingling sensation run up her body as she remembered the look in his eyes when he told her he had missed her. Could he be starting to care about her? Just the thought of him was causing a riot of emotions in her head and startling reactions from her body. Suddenly she realized that the sweat pouring from her skin was not totally caused by the hot bath. This physical sensation was foreign to her and scared her somewhat. *I'm acting like a lovesick schoolgirl,* she told herself. *He's just trying to be nice to me, and I'm blowing it all out of proportion.*

The matter settled, Penny completed her bath and wrapped the towel around her. Opening the door to let out the steam, she noticed Megan had left. A pretty peach-colored capri pant set was laid out on the bed. Penny put it on and admired the complement to her skin coloring the outfit gave her. She then proceeded to fix her hair. Finally, pleased with the image reflected in the mirror, she proceeded downstairs. When she reached the dining room, her aunt and Devin were already seated. Nodding to Devin, Penny took a seat next to Martha.

"My, don't you look pretty tonight," said her aunt.

"Thanks," said Penny, wishing for the hundredth time she could control the awful blush once again creeping up her neck.

Devin couldn't take his eyes off her, but he didn't say a word. Hoping for a compliment from him also caused Penny to be a little disappointed. Little could she know the dramatic effect she was having on the man across the table from her at that very minute.

Devin was shifting uncomfortably in his seat, trying to overcome a strong urge to go around the table, pull Penny into his arms, and give her a sound kissing. He knew she wasn't aware of how breathtakingly beautiful she was. The peach outfit brought out the highlights in her auburn hair and heightened her creamy complexion, giving it almost a rosy glow. Her eyes, when she looked up at him a moment ago, had deepened in color almost to black. He wasn't sure when he'd realized how much he had missed her, but this afternoon, when she had turned around and looked up at him, he knew he cared more than he wanted to admit. He had taken her abrupt departure up the stairs, however, as a rejection and was miffed with himself for showing his feelings to her. *I'll just keep my distance,* he told himself. *Megan can keep her company now that she's here. It will make my role as protector a lot easier.* Focusing his attention on the meal before him, Devin pushed his feelings to the dark recesses of his mind.

Unaware of the tension between the two young cousins, Aunt Martha kept up a constant conversation through the entire meal and also failed to notice their lack of appetite. She rose after finishing her meal and led them into the living room.

After a reasonable time, so as not to be rude, Penny excused herself and retired to her room, leaving Aunt Martha and Devin downstairs talking.

XI

Several days passed and a routine was established by Penny. In the mornings she would have breakfast with her aunt and help her in the kitchen, while learning to cook. She enjoyed their time together and looked forward to it each day. Megan also enjoyed horseback riding, so she and Penny would saddle up after lunch. They would ride in a different direction each day, exploring the countryside. This time together was conducive to getting to know each other and resulted in the two young women becoming very close.

Penny hadn't seen or spoken to Devin since the night of her return and took it for granted that he was busy with the farm in her uncles' absence. She would have been a little upset to know that Devin secretly accompanied them on their outings each day.

They thought they were alone, so the two young women shared many secrets of their lives, each comfortable in the knowledge that it would go no further than the other. Penny couldn't seem to help herself from asking Megan about Devin. She wanted to know everything about his childhood, his likes, dislikes, and so on. Megan didn't seem to mind the questions and answered each one willingly. Penny started to feel like she knew Devin a little better after each outing and found herself falling hopelessly in love with the young boy and man Megan brought to life for her each day. She didn't know that Devin could overhear some of their conversations. He had to stay close enough to the women to intervene in case of an emergency.

At first he was annoyed at being the main topic of conversation. He couldn't believe how willing Megan was to talk about him. After the first day or two, however, it dawned on him that all this inquisitiveness on Penny's part could only mean one thing. At least he hoped it did. He had just decided to halt Penny's inquisition of Megan by taking her off for the day himself, when Les, Ned, and his father returned.

Penny was ecstatic when she and Megan returned from their outing to find her aunt had returned. Jumping from her mount, she bounded up the porch steps and grabbed Les, nearly knocking the breath out of her.

"Whoa!" yelled Les. "You forget your strength, Pen!" Laughing, both the girl and her aunt hugged again.

Lesley pushed Penny back to arm's length and looked her over. "I see you've been faring okay. You look great, honey. It makes me kind of jealous, though, to see you look this good without any tender loving care from me."

"Oh, Aunt Les," laughed Penny, "I missed you terribly. I thought I would die when we came back from Sydney and you had left again."

"I figured as much and I'm sorry we had to do that, but a couple of more tests had to be run and right away. Let's not talk about that right now though; let's go inside and catch up."

Wrapping their arms around each other, the two women proceeded indoors, where a lively conversation was going on among Aunt Martha, Uncle Ned, and Uncle Dan. As soon as they stepped through the door, the talking stopped.

"Please continue," said Penny. "You'll make me think you're talking about us when you clam up like that," she laughingly commented.

The three adults exchanged guilty glances with one another before joining in Penny's laughter.

"Goodness, child . . .," broke in her uncles simultaneously. "You look like a different girl," continued her Uncle Dan.

"Yep," agreed Ned. "Looks like a change in country did you a world of good."

"I think you're right," agreed Penny. "I feel much better than I did, and I owe it all to Aunt Martha," she said, as she looked over and gave her aunt a wink.

Martha was beaming from ear to ear. "I'd have to say we helped each other," she said. "It's been great having Penny around."

The compliments and thanks continued on for a few more minutes as the family rehashed the events of the previous days. Aunt Martha filled the threesome in on all the details of Mandy's illness and what the doctors had found or, more correctly, hadn't found. The information seemed to dampen the spirits of Les, Ned, and Dan somewhat, but they drilled Martha for every detail. Just when Penny thought she would scream if Aunt Martha repeated herself one more time, Ben entered the room and announced dinner.

Devin came in and joined the party at the table. It was the first time since her arrival that Penny had been in the same room with him and she was a little subdued. Aunt Les questioned her about her activities and before long she was giving her aunt an animated detailed description of her daily romps through the countryside. Penny had broached the subject of the research and testing several times, but in each instance the conversation was subtly turned to other topics. Making a mental note to ask Les that evening when they were alone, Penny rejoined the current discussion.

Penny and Les retired around nine P.M. After showering and getting into her nightgown, Penny slipped next door to her aunt's bedroom. Knocking softly, she entered at Les's invitation.

Les looked like a teenager. Flushed from her bath and with her hair in a ponytail, she was sitting Indian style on the bed, putting cream on her face.

"What's up?" she asked.

"Aunt Les," Penny began, "is it my imagination or have you and my uncles been avoiding answering questions about your research?"

Les looked at Penny for a few seconds, weighing her answer. Her niece could tell from her expression that she was mulling something around in her mind. A decision apparently made, Les patted the bed for Penny to sit beside her.

"You will have to promise to keep what I'm going to tell you to yourself," she seriously stated. At Penny's nod, she continued. "Dan, Ned, and myself all agreed not to say anything to Martha in light of what she's been through already in the last couple of weeks." Les made herself a little more comfortable and continued. "This problem isn't just a case of a few sheep dying, Pen. It is very serious and lives, our lives, could be in danger."

After studying Penny's face for the impact of her words and apparently satisfied at what she saw, Les went on. "Ned has been conducting tests for the last couple of years on the water, grass, foliage, etc., surrounding the grazing area of the sheep. To give you a little more background and better understanding, about five years ago there was a drought here. This is not an unexpected occurrence and the ranchers are constantly preparing for these times. This particular year, however, the preparations were not enough. Uncle Dan lost nearly all his herd. After the devastation, Uncle Ned autopsied several of the carcasses and found everything to be normal except for the presence of a strange chemical he was not able to identify. Dan lost so many of his sheep that he had to sell off about half of the land to reinvest in a new herd. Since then, Ned has been conducting random testing throughout the ranch on the living and dying sheep. In every instance this substance, whatever it is, has been found. Ned has not been able to identify it yet.

"This last trip out we only tested the blood of the healthier sheep. Small amounts of this chemical, Ned has tagged it agent Y, were found in the samples. We compared this test to the tests done on the deceased sheep. The amounts of agent Y were five times greater in the dead sheep. Over the last few years, the area with agent Y has been growing. At first it was only found by the riverbed, on the eucalyptus and other plant life growing there. Now Ned had traced it to the water in the well here."

Penny broke in. "Les, maybe that is what made Mandy so sick!"

"This is the very reason why nothing can be said to Martha. Ned took samples from the well as soon as we returned and were told about Mandy. He had been testing the well water here for a couple of years now. Each time nothing was found until last week. That is why we immediately went back out to conduct several more studies. Penny, I can't divulge anything more right now. This is a lot more complicated than it appears to be. You have got to promise me not to say a word to anyone. As I said earlier, lives could be in danger here. Do you understand?"

Penny nodded silently.

"Now, do you have anything else you want to know?" asked her aunt, smiling at the very serious expression on Pennys' face.

"Nah," said Penny, jumping off the bed. She gave her aunt a hug and kiss and returned to her room.

Penny's mind was thinking in a million different directions at once. She could understand not wanting to upset

Aunt Martha with this information, but she couldn't comprehend the urgency and warning about lives being in danger. *Just who does Aunt Les think could be hurt?* she asked herself over and over again. Surely no one would want to hurt Aunt Martha, and she certainly didn't know anyone other than family. Could it be Devin, Uncle Dan, or Ned? Penny pondered her aunt's last words over and over into the night. Finally, in the wee hours before dawn, the young woman fell into a troubled sleep.

Les, however, was a lot more worried about the current situation than she had relayed to Penny. Dan and Ned had not wanted her to say anything to Martha *or* Penny about the test results. Les didn't agree with them and had decided to talk to Penny. They had all agreed what Les could relay and what she should keep from Penny.

Thinking back to her conversation with Dan over the phone several months ago, Les was unsure if she had done the right thing in bringing Penny here. A chemist for years, before quitting her job and moving in with Zack and Penny, she understood the importance for her presence here. The complete underlying danger of the venture hadn't been disclosed to her, though, until the night she and Penny arrived. Her first thought had been to repack and get the hell out of there, but Dan had made her promise to stay until talking to Ned. When Ned had disclosed his findings and the seriousness of the situation, she had no choice but to stay.

Talking to Penny that evening would alert her to the dangers they could be facing. She felt a little better knowing Penny handled pressure situations very well. They would have to leave again, day after tomorrow, and for how long she didn't know. She just hoped that with the three of them leaving to conduct the necessary testing and investigation, the danger to Penny would lessen. If anything happened to her—*No! I won't even let that possibility enter my head,* thought

Lesley, pushing the awful picture from her mind. Finally, mentally and physically exhausted, she too fell into a fitful sleep.

Neither woman would have been able to sleep if they had been aware of the events taking place just a short distance away from the house. A dark figure was making its way back into the wooded area surrounding the house. He had been outside Les's window eavesdropping on her conversation with Penny. His instructions were to find out how close the MaGraths were to identifying the chemical. From what he overheard, it sounded to him like they were very close to a discovery.

Scrambling down off the roof onto the ground, he let his guard down just long enough for another larger figure in the woods to pick him out. The larger man followed him for what seemed like hours, then slowed down and ducked behind a bush just as the smaller one turned around and peered into the darkness. The rooftop eavesdropper, satisfied that he hadn't been followed, let out a low whistle. Another shadow dislodged itself from the edge of the clearing and came toward him. Straining his ears, the man in the woods tried to make out the conversation, but could only hear a small portion. The two in the clearing abruptly split up, each going in different directions.

The larger man again followed the smaller one for a short distance. Suddenly a twig snapped under his foot. There was no time for stalling. The larger man reached the smaller one in just two strides. Reaching out, he grabbed the intruder and pulled him toward him. Getting a firm hold, the larger man twisted the smaller one's head, snapping his neck. Dropping the dead weight to the ground, he slipped back into the woods and disappeared.

XII

Penny awoke early the next morning surprisingly refreshed. By the time she got downstairs to the dining room though, everyone else was seated, leaving only the chair next to Devin vacant. Giving her a devilish grin, Devin patted the seat and told her he promised not to bite. She couldn't help but laugh at him, breaking the tension of the last couple of weeks.

Everyone was talking at once, making it difficult to really hear anything being said. Penny had to move closer to Devin to hear his conversation, causing her pulse rate to increase. She could smell his cologne, a woodsy-masculine scent, and felt she could stay in this position the rest of the day with no problem whatsoever.

Devin, however, was having a difficult time dealing with the closeness of the young lady, whose face was only inches away from him. Totally forgetting his earlier question to her, Devin returned her gaze. They were unaware that their behavior toward each other was not going unnoticed. Both Lesley and Martha had recognized the apparent fascination the two young cousins had for one another. However, their reactions to the discovery were quite different.

Martha was glad to see Devin finally interested in someone else. *He's going on with his life now, and it's about time,* she thought. Lesley was having a difficult time, however, knowing how innocent and vulnerable Penny was. Vowing to have a talk with her later that day, she continued to silently observe the young couple.

Suddenly realizing that Devin wasn't talking anymore, Penny abruptly pulled back. Embarrassed at her previous thoughts, she dropped her eyes to the plate of food in front of her. She had no appetite and proceeded to push the food around on her plate.

Devin, startled at Penny's reaction, smiled to himself. Maybe, just maybe, she was hiding her feelings for him. Time would tell, he thought and tackled his food with relish. Sneaking another glance at Penny and Devin, Aunt Martha almost laughed out loud. *This is going to be quite interesting,* she thought.

Les asked Penny to go riding with her after breakfast. Not wanting to put off the discussion with Penny concerning Devin, she felt the sooner it was out of the way the better. The two women left the house, unaware they were being followed. After riding for about an hour, they pulled into a clearing. There was a small cabin with a stream beside it. As much as Penny had been out the previous weeks with Devin and Megan, this was the first time she had seen this place. They dismounted and entered the small dwelling.

The only pieces of furniture were a wooden table and six chairs, a rocker, wood stove, and a wooden bed in the corner. Although the furnishings were sparse, the inside was spotlessly clean.

"Who lives here?" asked Penny.

"No one. This is just a rest station used by the herders now and then," answered Les. "Megan keeps it clean and well stocked for them. Sit down, Penny," instructed Les, anxious now for this talk to be over. Abruptly and to the point, she asked. "What are your feelings for Devin?"

Startled by the question and serious expression on her aunt's face, Penny started stammering. "Wh-what d-do you m-mean?"

"Penny, your feelings were written all over your face this morning. Your infatuation with Devin is very obvious. Has he made any advances toward you?"

Now completely at a loss for words and ashamed at being so easy to read, Penny started to tear up. Lesley was immediately sorry for her abrupt manner in handling the situation and moved toward the young girl, putting her arms around her. "Stop crying now. I'm sorry to upset you like this, but I have to know. Is Devin making passes at you or not?"

Penny didn't like the accusing tone her aunt was using, and totally unlike her normal self, pushed her away. She was getting a little angry herself and without warning exploded.

"No, he hasn't made any passes at me!" she finally shouted. "As a matter of fact, he has been a perfect gentleman and only doing what he had been instructed to do. If anyone is the blame, I'm the one at fault here, Aunt Les."

Les could see how fragile Penny's emotional state was right now. "I'm sorry, Pen. I just don't want you to get hurt."

"Aunt Les," said a now completely frustrated Penny, "I'm almost twenty-one years old. Most girls my age have had a dozen boyfriends and several serious relationships. I admit the feelings I have for Devin are somewhat new to me, but I really don't think they are anyone else's business but my own."

The two women stood inches apart, head to head, staring at one another. This was the first time Les could ever remember Penny standing up to her and expressing her feelings as an adult. It was difficult for her to accept, but she did, knowing Penny was right in what she was saying.

"It's hard for me to accept your being grown, Penny," said her aunt, an apology in her voice. "You're right. This is none of my business, and I'll try to keep my nose out of it, okay?"

"Oh, Aunt Les," sobbed Penny, more upset now at her aunt's apologetic manner than earlier. "I must really be making a complete fool of myself if you could see so easily how I feel about Devin."

"No, you aren't," Les reassured her, not ready at the moment to tell Penny what she'd also seen in Devin's expression that morning. "I love you, and, of course, I'm closer to you than anyone else. That's why I picked up on this like I did."

"Then you don't think Devin knows?" asked Penny hopefully.

"Of course not," lied her aunt.

"Good," said a relieved Penny. "He's been so nice and sweet to me, and I know Uncle Dan only kept him here to watch out for me. I tried not to care for him, I really did, but I can't seem to control myself." Les had to smile at the bewildered expression on Penny's face. "You don't have to worry though; this is a totally one-sided relationship," continued Penny.

Devin turned around and swiftly returned to his horse. He had come up to the cabin intending to join the women on their outing. Hearing the rising voices and then his name had caused him to stop in his tracks and listen. Now he was both glad and upset at what he heard. He understood the exhilaration he felt in the knowledge of Penny's feeling for him. What surprised him was the fear he also felt. *She'll just have to get used to me being around. I'll be like a second skin,* he vowed. Her safety would be his number-one concern. Nothing bad would happen to her; he would make sure of that.

Les and Penny left the small cabin and rode back to the house. Agreeing to meet after lunch for a game of chess, Penny continued on to the kitchen in search of Aunt Martha, while Les went up to her room.

Seeing her niece in the beginning stages of her first serious relationship, and this was definitely going to be one, she told herself, had unnerved her more than she cared to admit. What she'd seen this morning on Devin's face made her remember events that had happened in her own life at this same age in what now seemed eons ago. The memories were painful, but they had to be faced.

She had also been twenty when she had met Brent. They were both recently graduated chemists and had gone to work for the government. Zack had secured the position for Les through contacts of his.

Brent was a brilliant chemist with a wonderful future ahead of him. They had hit it off right away and were both elated when they were made partners in the Protoan project. They had worked day and night, side by side, until the project had been completed, several months ahead of schedule. As a bonus, the company had given them an all-expenses-paid leave to France. She remembered the fourteen glorious days they had spent getting to know one another.

They had fallen madly in love and had thrown caution to the wind, making wild passionate love every chance they got. Les still got emotional just thinking about it. After returning to work, they'd continued their daily routine.

About six weeks later, Les had started to get ill in the morning. She had started on the pill when they returned and dismissed the sickness as a side effect. Brent had been notified he was being transferred to the United States testing labs. He had asked her to marry him and together had planned a wedding as soon as he got settled in. She had accompanied him to the airport and watched the plane fly out of sight. When she had returned to the office that afternoon, their boss had informed her that Brent's plane had crashed and there were no survivors.

Les was crying freely now as all the events, so long ago, came crashing back on her. She had quit her job and fled to Zack's. They were very close, and he had always been her port in a storm. Still feeling sick a month later, she had discontinued the pills. When the nausea still didn't go away, and with Zack and Polly on her case, she went to a doctor. Les still remembered the diagnosis. "You're pregnant," the doctor had said, a big smile on his face. She had been terrified and ecstatic at the same time. She immediately knew she was going to have the child; but with no job or place of her own, she also knew the right thing to do would be to put the baby up for adoption.

She waited several days before telling Zack and Polly. Their reaction surprised her. Zack and Polly had tried to have children but couldn't. They were on the adoption agency list and had been for three years. She, Polly, and Zack talked into the wee hours of the morning. At the end it was resolved. Polly and Zack would adopt her baby and raise it as their own. Les would be Aunt Les, with input into the rearing of the child. It was a perfect solution and Les had jumped at it.

The day Penny was born Les had almost backed out. Seeing the adoration on Zack's and Polly's faces had changed her mind. She knew at that moment Penny would have a great life with Zack and she could share it. It was the best thing to do for Penny. So, through all the growing up years, Les had been there, taking an active part in the rearing of her daughter. Zack and Polly had been true to their promise and let her make decisions on Penny's behalf.

They were going to tell Penny, but then Polly became ill. Neither Zack nor Lesley wanted to hurt Polly, so it was put off until after she died. Then Zack had been so devastated after Polly's death, that Les hadn't had the heart to tell her then, so Penny had never been told. Sometimes it was extremely hard on Les, wanting Penny to know who she was, but she felt at this point in time it would do more harm than good.

Les snapped back to the present. The situation here between Penny and Devin would take very careful handling. She had nothing against Devin, but she did not want Penny hurt either. She had no choice. Penny had to accompany them when they left this time, or someone else would have to be left to watch over her. *Maybe I'm overreacting,* she thought to herself, then remembered the look on Devin's face this morning. *He is the most logical choice to protect her,* Les argued with herself. Penny's safety at this point was more important than her emotional status. Still arguing with herself, Les changed clothes and went downstairs to hunt for Penny.

XIII

A week had passed since Les's return. The trio were now packing for another excursion to the outback lab. Ned had informed them that he felt they were very close to isolating the mystery chemical. Just a few more tests needed to be done. Security was of the utmost importance, especially now. Les was still unsure of what she should do, if anything, about Penny, when the matter was taken out of her hands.

Martha wasn't feeling very well, and Penny was needed here to look after her. Martha had insisted it was just the flu when Ned voiced his hesitation at going himself. All agreed that Penny could run the household and look after her aunt. Devin would remain to watch over both women. Les wanted to stay this time but knew the importance of her expertise in these tests. She had also voiced her suspicions to her brothers on the identification of the chemical. Taking their leave the next morning, the threesome assured the housebound women that they would return before the week was out.

Penny was nervous at the responsibility put on her but, with newly found confidence, knew she was up to the challenge. She put her heart and soul into taking care of Martha and overseeing the household. Her aunt was really beginning to worry her when, after a couple of days, she didn't seem to be getting any better. The older woman hadn't been able to keep any nourishment down and was still running a high temperature. Against Martha's adamant objections, Penny called the doctor.

It took four hours for the man to get to the house. Martha was now slipping in and out of semiconsciousness. The doctor, who could not be much older than herself, Penny thought, was very concerned at Martha's current condition and immediately hooked her up to an IV solution. After asking Penny what seemed to be a hundred questions, he told her they needed to admit her aunt to the hospital.

Hearing the conversation taking place beside her bed, Aunt Martha roused herself long enough to vehemently refuse to go. Penny was now overwrought and terrified that her aunt might die. The doctor assured her, however, that with the right help and medicines, her aunt would pull through. "We'll need to have a nurse round the clock, though, to administer the medications," he informed her.

"Fine," replied the frightened girl. "Whatever is needed is fine."

Penny wished Les and her uncles would return early. She didn't like having the fate of her aunt lying solely on decisions she had to make.

The next few days passed in a blur of activity. The two nurses assigned to her aunt were in their late forties or early fifties. Both were no-nonsense types, concentrating solely on the care of their patient.

Penny's anxiety waned as her aunt started making positive steps toward her recovery. By the end of the week the nurses were no longer needed, and her aunt was her old happy self. Penny hadn't realized how tired and worn out she was until the emergency situation was over.

The first day Martha was out of bed and back into the kitchen, Penny excused herself and went up to her room. She had been sleeping on the chaise in Aunt Martha's room the last few nights, afraid to leave her. Now totally exhausted and relieved, Penny sat on the edge of the bed and fell back onto the pillows. She lay there, totally relaxed, and fell into the deep sleep of peace.

When Penny awoke, it was dark outside. *Boy, I must have died,* she chided herself. Taking a quick shower and donning her night clothes, she hurried downstairs to check on her aunt. Martha was in the recliner, watching TV.

"Well, I see the dead have come back to life," she said, laughing. "I sent Ben up to your room earlier to get you to eat lunch, but he said you were sleeping so soundly, he didn't want to wake you."

"Thanks, Aunt Martha. I didn't realize just how tired I was. Are you still feeling all right?"

"I'm fine, child. I'm just sorry to have put you through this whole ordeal," said her aunt, looking lovingly at the young girl beside her. Penny waved away her aunt's attempt at apology.

"I felt inept in handling the situation, though. You sure gave us a scare," said Penny, tears welling up in her eyes.

"Oh, bosh. Just gittin' older and taking longer to fight off these things, that's all," said Martha, wanting now to put the whole ordeal behind her. "I have supper warming in the oven for you. Come, I'll sit with you while you eat."

Penny noticed her aunt's labored breathing as they walked into the dining room.

"Are you sure you're okay? You haven't overdone it while I was sleeping, have you?" she scolded.

"No, I haven't, Momma," teased her aunt. "I guess I am weaker than I thought I was though. It will take me a little longer to get all my strength back, that's all. You are not to worry your head about me any more, you hear? As a matter of fact, I want you and Devin to go off somewhere tomorrow. Go fishing, picnicking, or something. You need a little time to yourself."

Penny refused her aunt's kind offer. "Not for a couple of days or so, Aunt Martha. I want to make sure you're fully recovered; besides, Aunt Les and Uncle Ned are supposed to be back by Friday. That's only a couple of days away. I guess you'll just have to put up with my continued nurse-maiding until then," she teased. Seeing the look of determination on her niece's face, Martha reluctantly gave in.

The next two days were peaceful ones. Penny and Aunt Martha went for walks and played cards. As each day passed, Penny grew closer and closer to the gentle, caring woman. The time together was also having an effect on Aunt Martha, kind of like another prescription, only for the heart. The young girl filled the vast emptiness left by her own daughter's death.

Friday came and went with no sign of Les, Ned, or Dan. Not unduly alarmed, Martha tried to convince Penny not to worry just yet. "Why, I've known your uncle to be several days late in coming back from his testing sites. In the outback you seem to lose all sense of time. They'll probably show up the first of the week not even aware that they've caused us to worry. I know just the thing to get your mind off of this. Go fishing tomorrow with Devin."

Seeing the objection forming on Penny's lips, Martha broke in. "No excuses. I'm fine now. You have seen with your own eyes that I'm fully recovered. You go have a good time, and I'll use the time to catch up on my reading."

Knowing any argument would be futile, Penny agreed, but not without apprehension. She hadn't seen or talked to Devin since her aunt was so ill and only then out of necessity and mutual concern. Realizing her aunt was right, she agreed. She needed to get away, if only for a few hours.

Martha set the trip in motion with Devin, unaware of the emotional turmoil this outing was causing him. He finally resolved himself to treating tomorrow as any other day on the job. He couldn't let his feelings for Penny get in the way of his role as her protector. On edge himself about the delay in his dad's return, he didn't want to alarm Martha or Penny. Call it a premonition or whatever, it just didn't feel right. He had already made up his mind to send out some of the farm workers to look for them if they didn't return by Monday.

The morning found the two young people in good spirits. Penny convinced herself to relax and just enjoy the fishing trip. Devin had lain awake the night before thinking about Penny. She was in his thoughts almost constantly now. Astounded by the intense feelings he had for her, he was equally determined to put them aside for the day.

Aunt Martha had packed a large basket, making them both promise to be careful and not to hurry. "Just be home before dark so I won't worry," was all she said. Penny was happy to see the rosy color back in her aunt's cheeks and the pep in her step once again.

The two young people didn't exchange small talk on the way to the lake, contented just to be in each other's company.

The lake was more beautiful than Penny had remembered. The misty fog had not completely lifted yet, seemingly in a duel with the sun's first rays. Penny watched, transfixed to the display before her. Slowly, the mist broke apart, letting beams of light hit the water below. As if on cue, fish started striking the surface. Water fowl swimming to the center of the lake suddenly separated, reminding Penny of the ice-skating ballet she and her dad had seen last Christmas. Not wanting to dwell on the event, still painful to her heart, Penny turned around and looked at Devin. "You ready to get skunked?" she teased.

"Don't think I have anything to worry about," he countered.

The playful banter continued between the two, as they settled down into chairs and concentrated on the serious business of fishing. After an hour of having not even one nibble, Penny talked Devin into walking around the lake.

"I never could sit still for very long," she confessed. "Used to irritate the heck out of Dad. He'd be quiet and still for hours at a time, while I wandered around all over the place. He'd get real peeved at me though when I'd come sit back down beside him, throw in the line, and catch one." Penny was laughing now, remembering the happy time.

Devin knew at that moment, without a doubt, the true depth of his feelings for her. She was looking up at him, relaxed and at peace for the first time in weeks, unaware of the tempting picture she presented. Her eyes were wide and innocent, but her smile was wholly provocative. He had to fight an impulse to grab her in his arms and silence her laughter with a kiss. Swallowing hard, Devin started walking a little faster. Penny had been able to keep up with him, stride for stride, until now. She found herself having to run to keep pace.

"Hey, are you trying to race or something?" she asked, stopping to catch her breath. It was Devin's turn to look embarrassed. Trying to cover up, he answered, "Got a hunger pang. It's a powerful one too. Beat you to the basket."

They both took off running. Penny had always loved a challenge and put a serious effort into beating Devin back, but he needed space from her at the moment and outdistanced her without even trying. The first back to the car, Devin had a minute to collect himself. If the remainder of the day was going to be anything like the last few minutes, he was not looking forward to it.

He knew Penny was unaware of her effect on him, and he wanted more than anything to let her know how he felt.

As she drew near, breathing hard, cheeks flushed, and sweat-soaked ringlets clinging to the sides of her face, Devin lost all his resolve, held out his arms, and gathered her into them. He could feel her heart pounding in her chest and her labored breath in his ear. His entire body was on fire. He wanted to lick the salt from her upper lip where beads of perspiration had popped out. Penny bent her neck back and looked up into Devin's eyes. What she saw was terrifying and wonderful at the same time. She loved the strength of his arms around her.

All at once the womanly feelings, dormant for so long, came flooding from her every pore. Hot, flushed, and excited, she lifted her lips to his in total abandonment. Devin could not contain himself any longer. He crushed her to him as he devoured her lips. Penny felt as though she were being consumed by flames. She wanted to melt into Devin's body and become one. A tingling sensation had begun in her upper thighs and was working its way up her torso. Burning all over now, Penny pulled back once more and looked once again into Devin's eyes, her own smoky black with desire. Shaken at her intense response, Devin took hold of her shoulders and pushed her back to arm's length. Fighting himself for control, he saw, too late, the hurt expression cross Penny's features. Before he could say anything, she tore out of his embrace and ran into the wooded area next to the car.

Devin knew the area well and was not concerned for her safety, but more than anything, he wanted to explain his hesitation. God knows he wanted to make love to her right then, but he also knew it wouldn't be right for her. He followed her into the woods.

Penny was humiliated! *What a fool I am,* she told herself, sobbing, as she ran away. She could hear him following her, but she wanted to escape the look she'd seen in his eyes.

She mistook his fight for control for revulsion. *He was actually trying to fight me off,* she told herself as she stumbled forward.

"Leave me be, please!" she cried, as Devin caught her arm and pulled her around.

"No, I won't," said Devin, gently trying to soothe her hurt pride. Penny was trying to free herself from his grasp but was held tight by his arms. "I'm not going to release you, so you may as well settle down and hear me out," he said, as calmly as he could..

Penny continued to squirm, but Devin held her tight until her struggles ceased. He lifted her chin up with his fingers and looked at the face of this childlike woman he loved beyond reason. Penny held her eyes closed, not wanting to look at him. She was mortified. *How could I have done such a thing?* she berated herself once again, bursting into a new flood of tears. Devin held her until her sobs subsided.

"Open your eyes, Penny," he finally demanded, his patience almost at an end.

Cautiously, hearing the change in his voice, Penny opened her eyes, one at a time. "I'm sorry I forced myself on you," she blurted out; but smiling, Devin quieted her outburst with a gentle kiss.

Now finally commanding her full attention, he calmly announced, "I love you."

Penny gazed up at him as the words and their meaning slowly penetrated her consciousness. "But I thought—" she began once again.

"Hush and let me finish," he said, as he held her tight. "I know what you thought, and you can see now that you were wrong. This is not the place for me to show you just how much I love you. You'll just have to take my word for it, okay?" Bending once again toward her, he took her lips in a kiss, then tore himself away.

Penny felt like she would explode with happiness. The look of pure love she gave him at that moment almost caused him to change his mind. "Come, let's go back," he managed to croak. Arm in arm, they returned to the lake.

XIV

When Les, Dan, and Ned had returned to camp, they found it had been ransacked. Before now, they had only guessed at the danger involved, but now all knew it was indeed a life-threatening situation they were dealing with here. Determined more than ever to break down the identity of this chemical, they all started the cleaning process.

Earlier, on the way back, they had all discussed how much easier it would be to have the samples brought back to them at the complete laboratory Ned had at home. The camp's destruction affirmed the decision to keep this away from Martha and Penny.

It took the entire first day to reassemble the portable lab and accommodations. Tired from their trip out and cleaning activities, all three decided to retire and get an early start in the morning.

It was raining when they rose and continued for the next two days, putting all of the trio in a rather bad humor. Les had decided to return home the next morning if she awoke to another downpour. They were all pleasantly surprised, however, to find the sun shining bright and cheerful the next day. The rain had left everything smelling fresh and clean. By the end of the day, everyone was again in good spirits, having collected enough samples to hopefully give them the answer they needed so desperately. After sorting the various vials and labeling them, the group started adding different chemicals to each one. The results would take forty-eight hours, which gave each of them time to read, explore, or just loaf. It was getting close to midnight by this time and they were bone tired.

Les entered her tent, unzipped the sleeping bag on her cot, and climbed in. Before her head touched the pillow, she was asleep. Ned and Dan continued talking until the wee hours of the morning, finally turning in around three.

Les awoke to a raging headache. It took several hours and a couple of doses of aspirin to get rid of it. They all were impatient for the tests to be over, each for different reasons. Dan wanted an answer once and for all as to what was killing his sheep. Ned was very concerned at finding traces of the unidentified chemical in his well water. Something had to be done to counteract it; but until they knew what it was, their hands were tied.

Les was puzzled. She hadn't mentioned to her brothers yet that she had recognized the properties identified in the substance so far but couldn't put her finger on its name. She had wracked her brain after each test had come back with the expected results. Familiar though it was, she could still not identify the chemical or remember where or when she had dealt with it before. Feeling especially frustrated and drained from the headache, she decided to walk down by the river's edge.

She thought back to her conversation with Penny just a few days ago. It still bothered her to leave Penny with Devin; but until this mystery was solved, she had no choice. She had made up her mind that as soon as they could, they would return to the U.S. Penny needed to go on to college and get a degree. As far as she knew, the young girl had no idea of what career she wanted to pursue. Zack had babied Penny a little too much for Les's liking, but she hadn't had the heart to stop him. She wouldn't be around forever though, and Penny had to be able to take care of herself. Les's thoughts flitted from one thing to the other, when all of a sudden she knew without a doubt why all the test results were so familiar to her. Oh, my God! She groaned to herself. Jumping up and spinning around, she was caught off guard. Too late she held up her arm to shield the blow that plummeted her into blackness.

XV

Penny and Devin were inseparable for the next couple of days. Aunt Martha looked at the two young lovers with a touch of sadness. She was extremely happy for them both, but she couldn't help thinking of the life and love her own daughter was missing. Determined not to let her feelings cloud their happiness though, she put her sad thoughts from her mind.

Devin and Penny were returning from their afternoon horseback ride and noticed Aunt Martha pacing out in front of the house..

"What's the matter?" asked Penny, her concern very apparent in her voice.

"I've got this feeling, just can't explain it," said her aunt. "Devin, I think it's time you went out to the camp. Probably nothing is wrong, but they're three days overdue now and I'm getting a little worried."

Devin jumped down from his saddle and tied his horse to the fence. "I have to admit, Martha, it doesn't feel right to me either. I haven't said anything to you because I'd already made up my mind to leave tonight."

"Good, come inside and eat a bite; then you can be on your way."

Seeing the abrupt no-nonsense attitude of her aunt fully alarmed Penny. "Do you think something has happened to them?" she asked nervously.

"I really don't know what to think, child," answered her aunt. "All I do know is that we should have heard something from your uncles or someone by now. Ned's never been this overdue without contacting me some way. He knows how worried I become. No, something's not right. Something's just not right," muttered her aunt as she went up the steps.

Penny remembered the last time her aunt said almost the same words. Now she felt a little sick to her stomach. "Please, God, protect Aunt Les," she kept saying to herself, over and over.

Devin ate very little, now anxious to be on his way, but he packed enough food to carry with him to make up for it. Penny wanted to go with him, but he firmly refused.

"Hopefully everything is okay and they are just so engrossed in the research, they have forgotten about us. If that's it, I'll be back by Thursday evening. If there is a problem of some kind, I'll be back as soon as I can. I will let you know either way. Martha, keep Ben close to you and be very aware of everything that's going on around you," Devin cautioned.

Penny looked at her aunt and saw she was nodding her head to Devin's instructions.

"Please be careful," was all she could say, before Devin pulled her to him.

"Penny," he said, looking seriously into her face, "I love you. Now listen carefully. I want you to stay in the house with Martha until I get back. Promise?"

Penny nodded her head, trying hard not to release the tears threatening to overflow at any minute.

"Penny, I mean, in the house, not back in the gazebo or in the woods or anything. *In the house,* do you understand?" Still nodding her head up and down Penny realized how frightened Devin was for their safety.

"I'll stay inside, Devin, I promise," she reassured him.

After giving her one last crushing kiss, he jumped into the Jeep and sped away.

Aunt Martha and Penny returned to the house and retreated into the living room. Martha could tell Penny needed to talk to someone, so she started a seemingly innocent conversation with her troubled niece.

"We haven't spent much time together the last few days and I know I'm selfish in saying this, but I've missed your company."

Penny was not expecting this line of conversation and it took her completely by surprise. "I'm sorry, Aunt Martha. We didn't mean to leave you out. Everything has been happening so fast. I feel like I have been on a roller coaster. Between Dad's death, our trip over here, and all the wonderful people I've met, then Mandy's illness and recovery, my feelings for Devin, which I'm still trying to understand, and now this, Aunt Martha, it's been up and down, up and down. Nothing seems to be stable anymore."

Martha looked at Penny with sympathy and understanding. She had ridden that emotional roller coaster herself not too long ago.

Leaning forward as if to give more meaning to her words, Penny continued. "When Mom died, I felt a great sadness. I was actually glad when the end came, for I knew it ended all her pain. I felt guilty for months for feeling that relief. I never discussed Mom's sickness or death with Dad. He was emersed in his own private hell, and I didn't want to bother him. Aunt Les was always closer to me really, than Mom, but I couldn't talk to her about this because I felt like I was betraying Mom somehow with my closeness to Aunt Les. From the time Mom died til we moved to Florida, I felt like I had lost both parents. Dad would sit as if in a daze for hours. I would talk to him, but he wasn't there with me; he was with Mom. You know, Aunt Martha, I almost started hating my mother then." Penny took a deep ragged breath.

Martha wanted to tell her it was okay, but she knew Penny had to talk it out, get it out of her system.

"When Dad came home and told Aunt Les and I that he had found a place in Florida *and* bought it, well, I was so happy. Daddy was his old self, laughing, excited, and ready to start living again. It was wonderful having him back. We were a close, happy family again, Me, Aunt Les, and Dad." She paused for a moment, then continued. "I was the one who found Daddy, Aunt Martha," she said, her voice cracking.

Martha nodded her head, not wanting to interrupt the steady flow of words her niece needed to say. "I found him, but you know, I still can't convince myself he's dead. I never even got to see him at the funeral home. A closed casket is what he'd requested in his will. You know, he never told me he wanted a closed casket. It's been so strange. I wake up in the morning sometimes ready to run downstairs and have coffee with him; then I remember he's not there. If anything happens to Aunt Les—Oh, God, please don't let anything happen to Aunt Les." Penny covered her face with her hands and shook with sobs. The tears she had denied herself for so long would not be stilled.

Martha pushed her bulk out of the recliner and sat beside the grieving girl. Pulling her close to her chest, she soothed Penny like she used to soothe Angela, gently rocking her back and forth.

XVI

Devin knew it would take the rest of the afternoon and early evening to get to camp. He tried not to think about what he might find, but thought instead of the last couple of days spent with Penny. If anyone had told him a month ago that he would be in love with someone, he would have called them crazy. The truth was, he was head over heels in love with her. The last few days they had gone horseback riding, picnicking, fishing, and just walking, all the while getting to know more and more about each other. He had opened up to her as if he had known her all his life. She was gentle, innocent, caring, and so at ease and at home in the outback. She didn't seem to mind that all they had to occupy their time together was rather primitive entertainment. He had asked her on several occasions over the last couple of days if she was bored. He would have taken her into town to a show, dinner, or dancing, although he himself didn't really look forward to the prospect. Relieved and happy when she declined made him appreciate her all the more. They had shared their life stories with one another, and he probably knew more than anyone else just how much Lesley meant to Penny.

Dusk was approaching and he turned on the headlights. The air was getting cooler and had a crisp, clean scent to it. Devin had packed his revolver and had it lying on the seat next to him. He was very much aware of the danger he could be entering and that thought in itself helped keep his mind alert to the surrounding environment. The land rolled by and Devin's brain was ticking along as fast as the mileage on the odometer.

He and Ben had discovered Frank, his uncle's handyman, in the clearing behind the house yesterday morning. He had died apparently from a broken neck. They had agreed to keep the secret between themselves so as not to alarm the women. Ben thought they should call the police, but Devin had persuaded him to wait until Ned returned. Now he wasn't sure if he had done the right thing. *I guess it depends on what I find out here,* he told himself. He knew the importance of the secrecy surrounding the tests his father was conducting. *I did what I had to given the current situation,* he reassured himself. *Anyway, I'll know what I'm facing pretty soon now.*

He was only about an hour away when his headlights picked up something lying in the middle of the road. Slowing down, he picked up the revolver then put it back when he identified the body as another one of the sheep. *Won't be long now,* he told himself. The dead sheep had alerted him once again, however, to the reason for his being out here. Clearing his mind of all other thoughts, mainly Penny, he concentrated solely on the road ahead.

All he could see now was the ground immediately in front of the truck illuminated by the twin beams. Every now and then he caught a glimpse of a wombat. These nocturnal animals were prevalent in this area so close to the river. He had liked to watch them playing in the mud as a child.

He was beginning to think they had moved the camp when the headlights picked up the outline of one of the tents. Strange, he thought, no campfire or lanterns were lit. He immediately turned off the headlights and cut the engine. Slipping out of the front seat, he grabbed the revolver and dashed into the darkness surrounding the camp. After going several feet, he stopped and listened. Nothing. There was no sound of anything other than the flow of the river very close to him now.

His eyes adjusted to the dark and he could once again make out the outline of the dark tents. Crouched down and moving slowly and silently, he came back toward the camp. Again he stopped and listened, hearing nothing. He approached the first tent. Looking to the left and right, he brought himself up to the front opening. It was unzipped, allowing him to slip inside unhampered. Once inside his eyes adjusted to the darkness of the interior. He could make out the cot and a couple of backpacks. This was apparently Ned or his father's tent. Men's boots were under the cot, seemingly awaiting the return of their owner. Finding nothing amiss, he slipped out and headed to the next tent. Once inside, the picture it presented was totally different than the previous one.

The floor of the tent was scattered with clothes and papers. Someone had been hurt, he surmised, finding a small pool of blood over by the small cot. His heart was racing now, every sense alert. This had to be Les's tent. Her hairbrush was tossed into the middle of the array of clothes.

The hair was standing up on the back of his neck when once again he exited the tent. He decided to hide the truck and himself until morning. Finding his way back, he cautiously looked inside before getting in. He left the headlights off as he started the engine. Backing up the road, he turned off the main lane into the thick brush, away from the river. His mind was bogged down with dread. He knew nothing could be done until morning. He would just hide the truck and find a place to rest until first light. He knew just the spot to be totally camouflaged.

Driving slowly, Devin eased his way to an old dry spring bed quite a distance away from the camp. He hoped his memory was accurate, as driving without headlights was working on his already taut nerves. He found the bed with minimal trouble and backed the Jeep under an overhanging tree.

Backtracking on foot as far as possible, Devin obliterated the Jeep's telltale tire tracks. Then, making himself as comfortable as possible, he settled back in the seat. Ears and eye straining to pick up all sights and sounds, Devin thought about what he had seen when he entered the tents. His father's and Ned's had shown no signs of struggle. Les's, however, was a different story. There was no sign of a struggle, but it was very apparent someone was looking for something before they left. The blood on the floor had him worried though. It could have been tracked in or dropped; part of one of the tests, he tried to reassure himself. Where in the world were they, though? He knew his dad always carried a firearm for protection, as did Uncle Ned. Whoever was responsible for their disappearance had to have surprised them all. Les was the one he was most concerned about. The blood pooled on the tent floor still bothered him. All he could do was speculate, and he knew from past experience this was a foolhardy thing to do. He had to plan what he was going to do in the morning. So Devin concentrated on his next step, which was what?

All the confusion of the last hour or so came crashing in on him full force. Who in the world was he facing? All his dad had indicated to him in the past was that he was dealing with unscrupulous people. Evidently, that was the understatement of the year. Devin had no idea where to begin to look for them. He certainly couldn't charge in anywhere by himself, so his first priority was to get help, but from whom? The only person, other than Dan, Ned, and family, was Ben. He thought of Kathy and Kit, but they had the kids to worry about. *Who in the hell as I going to get to help me?* he asked himself over and over again.

The only answer was Ben, Penny, and Aunt Martha. He was hesitant to even ask their hired help for fear they might also be involved in this. *The only thing I can do is return to Ned's in the morning and maybe, between all of us, a solution will present itself.* He hated to involve the women, but then decided it would be the best thing for all of them to stick together. *First light, I'll return,* he finally decided.

Devin strained to listen to all the sounds. Nothing but the usual night animal voices filtered in. He had only a couple of more hours before sunrise.

The sound of a gunshot jerked him awake. The sun was just coming over the rise. A fog had rolled in and visibility was minimal. Devin held his breath, afraid to let even his breathing make a sound. He had to pinpoint where the sound had come from before he made any moves. There! another shot. From what he could determine, they had come from the direction of the camp. He knew he could start the Jeep and not be heard from that distance.

Cranking the engine, he slowly made his way out of the cover of the tree. Taking the back trails for quite a distance, so he wouldn't be seen on the main road, Devin made his way back toward Ned's. Saying a silent prayer that everything back there would be all right, he pulled back on to the main road, only after assuring himself that no one had noticed him. Now to get back to Penny and Martha. *Please, let them be safe* was all he could think the whole way back.

XVII

The pounding, Les assessed, was her own heartbeat in her ears. Pain, excruciating pain, came in waves, making her sick to her stomach. She tenderly touched the spot on the back of her head where the pain seemed to be originating from. Someone had put gauze on it. The effort of trying to sit up was too much for her though and she slumped back down on the cot. Slowly, she inched open her eyes. Expecting light, she was surprised to see herself in a dark room, a pretty small room at that. The only piece of furniture was the cot she was lying on. There was one door and not a single window. A small lamp was on the floor by the door, its beam just breaking up the darkness. Trying to remember what happened seemed to be too much for her and she slipped back into unconsciousness.

In the next building, Dan was having a hard time dealing with the closeness of his room. He and Ned had been surprised and overtaken at the camp two days ago. They had finished up the last test and were discussing the implications of the results when several armed men had appeared out of the thick brush. He had started to run to the tent to get his gun but was quickly overtaken by them. They were bound and gagged and ushered into a van. Just before the doors closed, he got a glimpse of two men carrying a very limp Lesley. They had entered her tent, hampering his view of her. Enraged, he pushed toward the door, only to have it slammed in his face and locked. He and Ned looked at each other, but talk was impossible with the gags in their mouths.

All he could think about all the way here was how bad had Lesley been hurt.

They rode for what seemed like hours. Then the van stopped and the doors were thrown open. Several men had grabbed him and Ned and pushed them through huge wooden doors. On each side of the hall were more doors, one after another, reminding him of the rooms in the hospital, only smaller. About halfway down the hall, the men stopped and opened up the door to one of the rooms. They pushed Ned through that one and immediately locked it. They continued down three more doors, Dan counted them, then opened another. They roughly pushed him into the room, causing him to trip and fall. His hands were freed and the door slammed shut before he could get back up.

He was in total darkness. When his eyes had adjusted enough to see, he made out a cot along one wall. A small battery-powered lantern was beside the door. He removed the gag from his mouth and crawled over to the lamp. He was surprised that the lamp lit up when he turned it on. The room was all wood. The cot was the only furnishing, except for a five-gallon bucket in the far corner, which he correctly surmised was the toilet. He yelled for Ned.

"Yeah, are you okay, Dan?"

"Fine, I'm more worried about Les. Did you notice anything on the way in here?"

"Three maybe four more buildings like this one. Pretty big compound here. Any ideas what this is?"

"No, I sure don't. We've got to figure a way out of here though. Les was hurt, that much I could tell. We've got to find some way to help her."

The conversation ended on that note, while both men fell deep in thought.

After what seemed like hours, Dan heard a door being opened and then shut.

"Ned!"

"It's not mine," was his brother's response. In a few minutes, the lock on his door jiggled and the door was opened.

Dan stood in front of the door, ready to knock down the intruder. The door was flung open and a rifle jammed into his chest. He immediately backed away. The man holding the rifle smiled. He stepped aside as another man, vaguely familiar to Dan, stepped into the small room.

"We're sorry for the roughness with which you had to be taken," said the man, without an ounce of apology in his expression. "In due time you will be informed of your reasons for being here. Until then, I advise you to be quiet, do as you are told, and don't give us any reason to harm you." With this last sentence, the man gave a small smile.

Dan did not take too nicely to being bossed around and once again started forward. The man with the rifle lowered it toward him.

"Please, take heed of the seriousness of your situation here and listen to my instructions. You will be filled in on what you need to know soon enough," said the second man, as he backed out of the room.

"My sister," yelled Dan, "what about my sister? She's hurt. Where is she?" he pleaded.

"Your sister is fine. We have her in another area. You will all be reunited in due time. Your meals will be brought in to you, and your bathroom, as you can see, is in your room. You will be taken outside as we see fit. Until later then?"

Dan watched the man leave and the door close after him. He wanted to punch the smirk off the man's face but realized the stupidity of the thought. It would take a lot of will power for him to survive in this little room with nothing else short of breathing to do.

117

After hearing the door once again close, he and Ned started talking. They kept up a lively conversation for quite a while. Finally, nervous exhaustion overtook each of them, and they both lay down on their cots.

XVIII

Penny and Aunt Martha had decided to sleep downstairs in Martha's bedroom. Her aunt had convinced Penny that they needed to be close together in case of any emergency. Penny didn't need much convincing and was all too ready to comply with her aunt's wishes.

After showering and dressing for bed, both women propped up in the huge master bed and exchanged small talk, just like two schoolgirls, until after midnight. Aunt Martha shared stories with Penny about her father's and her aunt's childhood. She hadn't laughed so hard in a long time. Her aunt brought to life the adventurous antics of her dad and the tomboyish games of her aunt. Saying a prayer for her aunt and uncles safe return, Penny finally turned over and drifted off to sleep.

Martha, however, was still wide awake. She knew in her bones that something was very wrong. She also knew that if Ned, Dan, and Lesley were in danger, so were she and Penny. Through the day she had made plans for her and the child's safekeeping, if it was needed. The sleeping girl beside her had been sent by God, she now believed, to help her in dealing with Angela's death. Penny had become very dear to her in this short period of time. There was no way, as long as she lived, that any harm would come to her.

Martha smiled down at her niece. Just about ready to settle down herself, she reached over and turned off the lamp. The door to the room cracked open ever so slowly. Totally alert now, Martha eased off the side of the bed. In the darkness she could make out Ben's outline. He was motioning that they had visitors.

Martha surprised herself at how calm she was handling the situation. She knew exactly what they had to do. Reaching over and turning the lamp's on switch backwards, she and Ben watched as the panel that made her bed's headboard slowly and silently descend to the floor. The wall in back of the headboard slowly opened inward. Gently shaking Penny and holding her hand over her mouth, Martha motioned for her to slip onto the treadmill-like opening of the passageway. Penny, terrified, but instantly alert to the present danger, climbed into the opening and felt herself being lowered into the interior. Martha, surprisingly agile for her size, followed her niece. Ben hit the switch once again on the light and swiftly followed the women as the panel of the headboard and the wall opening slowly closed behind him.

The odor was somewhat musty but not unpleasant. It reminded Penny of a mixture of old wood and flowers. This surprised the girl as the escalatorlike apparatus continued to lower the threesome to the hideaway. As they got closer to the bottom, Penny saw another wall open up as they continued into a huge underground room. As soon as Ben had cleared the second wall, he jumped off the lift and hit the button on the side of the wall. Immediately this wall also closed.

Reaching bottom, Penny stood up and looked all around. Martha had climbed down off the wooden platform and straightened out her night clothes.

"Well, here we are, child. Our home for however long it needs to be," she said.

For once in her life, Penny was speechless. The room had several lanterns, which Ben lit, casting off eerie shadows. It was chilly and Martha quickly turned on the oven of the big stove in the corner. In no time at all the chill had gone.

There were two big couches, a dining table and six chairs, two single beds, and a refrigerator. There was a partition in the corner, and after a quick inspection, Penny found a small bathroom.

"Aunt Martha?" was all Penny got out before her aunt started to chuckle at the bewildered expression on the girl's face.

"When Ned and I built this house, the land was somewhat untamed and all manner of men lived out here. Ned was gone quite a lot and was constantly worried for mine and the kids' safety. So he and Ben built this room. It took quite a while and the only time I've ever had to use it is now. Ned would be proud at how well we escaped!"

Penny still looked puzzled, so Martha continued. "Ben saw men approaching the house. We had already agreed several days ago to come down here if needed. Ben has stocked lots of groceries, as you can see, so we won't starve. The stove and fridge are gas, as are the lanterns. The intruders upstairs can search all they want. Once the panel in the headboard went back into place, there is no way they can find us."

"How long will we stay down here?" asked Penny, her voice now quivering as the realization of the true danger they were in sank in.

"Ned and Dan know where the passageway is, although Devin does not. Until one of them comes and says all is well, here we stay."

"What if they never come?" asked Penny, her voice cracking as she talked.

"Don't even think that way, child! One of them will come, but we aren't trapped down here. There is another way out behind the fridge. If it takes longer than I think it should, Ben can leave and check things out. In the meantime, get some sleep. I'm afraid we're in for a long wait."

Above the threesome, the intruders were indeed very much surprised to find no one asleep in the bedroom. The man upstairs had also watched their approach. He was now as baffled as the rest.

"What do you mean you saw no one leave?" they shouted at one another. "They just didn't disappear into thin air. The boss ain't going to like this at all. Nosiree, not at all." They searched the house one more time from top to bottom, to no avail, and left. None of them were looking forward to telling "B" of the disappearance of the house's inhabitants.

Penny, Martha, and Ben spent a restless night. The women had slept on the beds, while Ben sacked out on the couch, but only after they had all sat and talked until early morning. Penny was very afraid, especially now, for Devin. Aunt Martha had mentioned that Devin was not aware of this room. They had agreed to stay below for a least forty-eight hours. If Devin found Ned, Dan, and Les and returned, Ned would know where to find them. If he didn't find them, well—they all hated to even let that thought flitter through their minds. If no one had come by the forty-eight-hour time limit set, then Ben would go out by the exit behind the fridge. The tunnel came out back behind the gazebo, well hidden in the trees.

Martha had suggested that Penny read to pass the time. A good supply of paperbacks were in a small bookcase by the beds.

The room was cozy in a way. It was the size of the living room and dining room combined. It was comfortable too after the oven had eliminated the chill. After tossing and turning for what seemed like hours, Penny decided to just get up. Martha had finally gone to sleep and Ben was snoring loudly. Tiptoing over to the bookcase, she selected a book by an author she had never heard of. It was a mystery-romance and, hopefully, would be interesting enough to wile away some of the time. She had read a couple of chapters when Aunt Martha started to stir. Ben immediately was on his feet. Penny smiled to herself as she watched the wizened old man help Martha get coffee and breakfast going.

"You hungry?" asked her aunt.

"Famished," was Penny's honest reply.

"Well, grab a cup for the coffee. Eggs and toast will be done in a sec."

Penny uncoiled her long legs from beneath her, went over to the stove, and filled her cup with the steaming hot brew. Boy, was it good. She could feel the warmth from the hot liquid spread through her entire body.

"How's the book?" asked Martha, as she artfully flipped the pan of eggs.

"Pretty good, I guess, although I'm having a difficult time concentrating on what I've read. Not to change the subject or anything, but will we be able to hear if anyone comes into the house?"

"I'm afraid not, child. We built this room to be sound-proof. Remember, when we did this, the kids were young. We didn't want anyone to hear them if we had to use this room. Just as well. It's nerve-wracking for us, but at least we can turn on the stereo and talk in a normal voice without fear of being heard."

"I guess you're right," agreed Penny, settling back once again on the couch. "I'm just a little claustrophobic."

"We'll all be about to climb the walls, I reckon, before this is over," replied her aunt, as she sat down at the table with her full plate of eggs and pan-fried toast.

Silence followed as the threesome concentrated on the hot food before them.

XIX

Devin felt the hair prickle on the back of his neck. It was too quiet as he drove into the yard. Upon entering the front hall, he could immediately see the overturned tables and went into the living room. The huge bookcase had been torn to pieces. The rugs were pulled here and there. He retreated back into the hall and over to the dining room and kitchen. It was the same story in those rooms. His heart was pounding in his chest as he continued his search into his aunt's bedroom. It had been destroyed. The big master bed had been pulled out from the wall, the mattresses stripped and hanging over the sides. All the drawers had been ransacked. He was afraid of what he might find, but knew he had to check the upstairs.

Saying a silent prayer, he began the climb. All the doors were open. After checking each room completely, he descended once again to the lower floor. At least no one was dead or hurt. That had to be a good sign. But now he had to revamp his plans on finding Les, Ned, and his dad. He had to also assume that the same people now had Martha and Penny. He had no choice but to call Kit and Kathy. They were the only family he had left who hadn't disappeared into thin air. He was afraid to contact the authorities; it was very clear that he not hang around here.

Going back into the kitchen, he found some juice and bread. Grabbing a glass off the counter, he poured it full and bent the bread around some cheese he also found in the fridge. Devouring his snack, he backtracked upstairs.

Stuffing more clothes into a backpack and grabbing his rifle from the closet, he got back into the Jeep.

After thinking a minute, he had decided to go back home. Acting without thoroughly thinking this out would be foolish. Besides, he knew who he could and could not trust on his ranch.

Without another moment's hesitation, he put the vehicle in gear and drove off. The entire ride home was filled with thoughts of his family and Penny, especially Penny. He had to clear his head of all the awful images that kept creeping into his mind. *I can't allow myself to think these things,* he kept telling himself. *I'll find them all; that's all I need to focus on at this point. It sure would help if I knew what I was dealing with though.*

Hopefully, his dad had confided in Myree. That was really his only hope at this point. His father had always trusted Myree with everything. If anyone could direct him on what to do next, it would be her. "If only it wasn't so damn far," he cussed under his breath. The rest of the journey home was filled with a turmoil of emotions playing in his heart and his mind. By the time he finally reached his destination, he was emotionally and physically exhausted.

Myree had been summoned by her granddaughter at Devin's arrival. Meeting the young man at the top of the porch stairs, she made a quick assessment of his physical and mental state. Calling Megan, she sent her out to find Kurt. Then she led Devin to the dining room, where a steaming hot bowl of stew was waiting. Devin sat down and devoured the delicious meaty dish in just a few minutes. That bowl was replaced immediately with another one just like it. His appetite appeased enough to talk while he ate, he then proceeded to fill Myree in on the events of the last few days. By the time he had recounted everything leading up to his arrival, he was once again in a very agitated state. Myree put an arm on his shoulder and persuaded him to once again take his seat and finish the meal.

"Looks to me like you need to map out a plan with someone you can totally trust," said the old woman in a matter-of-fact way. As Devin nodded his head while he continued to eat, she calmly continued. "Megan knows these here parts and so does Kurt. You know you can trust Megan with your life. You know more about Kurt than I do." Nodding in agreement, Devin knew the truth in her words.

"There are also many of the hands who have worked with and for your dad for many years. First, though, before you take any action, I think you need to get a couple of hours rest." Holding her hand up to still the denial on Devin's lips, she proceeded, "You won't be any help to anyone in your present state, Dev. Kurt and Megan can be packing what gear is necessary and getting you all road ready. I'll wake you in no more than three or four hours. You need at least that to be able to go on."

Seeing the wisdom in Myree's words, Devin had to agree; although after the refreshing meal he had just eaten, he felt that he could leave right this minute and not lose precious hours sleeping. Myree wouldn't be denied however and finally convinced the young man to lie down.

Filling Kurt and Megan in on the situation at hand, she turned them loose on getting supplies and gear packed for the trip. The old woman was hiding very well the anxiety she was feeling. She had raised Dan, Zack, and Les. It had just about killed her when she learned of Zack's death. She couldn't even allow the thought of the other two, so close to her heart, not coming back home. Devin was a level-headed young man. She could tell by the end of his story, however, that he was in love with Penny. Kurt and Megan would add the levelheadedness needed for this venture to have a positive ending. She had told Devin that she trusted Megan and

Kurt with his life. That was really half true. Megan, yes. Kurt, she hoped so.

Now she had to sit down and think where would be the place to hide people from the rest of the world. Myree was all too familiar with the outback. Living here all her life, she had been over just about every square inch of this continent. Getting out her well-worn map and drawings, she spread them out on the dining room table and concentrated on studying every line. Before it was time to wake Devin, she was sure that between Kurt, Megan, and herself they would know where to look.

Just then Megan and Kurt returned to the house. The young lady, weather-bronzed young man, and wizened old woman bent their heads to the task at hand.

XX

Les could hear someone calling her name, but it sounded like the person was in a tunnel. Her head ached and her ears felt like they had a ton of wax in them. Ever so slowly she inched her eyelids open. As the light entered, the pain intensified. She heard someone's voice, this time a little clearer, saying her name. Forcing herself to open her eyes, she looked at the face leaning over her. At first it was hard to get it in focus, then little by little the face came together. The man was asking her if she was okay. "Are you hurting?" he kept asking over and over.

She must have died. That had to be it, she told herself as she gazed into Brent's icy blue eyes. She never really thought she would actually see him in heaven, especially so lifelike. In her religious training she was taught that you left your physical body behind when you died and only your spirit went to heaven. Well, that was certainly wrong. She liked this. This was wonderful! If it weren't for that gosh-awful banging pain in the back of her head, she would be ecstatic! Making an effort to talk, she opened her mouth and tried, but nothing came out except a moan. Brent was putting a cool cloth on her forehead. Wait a minute, what was he saying? Trying to focus, Les strained to hear.

"Why the hell did you hit her so hard! I told you not to hurt her; she's too important for us and to this project. The lump on the side of her head is the size of an egg. We'll be lucky if her skull isn't fractured." Turning back and looking down at Les, he called her name once again.

"Les, can you hear me? Squeeze my hand. Blink your eyes. Anything, just let me know you hear me."

Les continued to stare up at the handsome apparition above her. But wait, something was very wrong; she could sense it. Before she said anything, she wanted to figure it out in her mind. Sure now that she wasn't dead, she pretended not to hear Brent. Maybe she was hallucinating or dreaming. His voice was so real though, and she felt the cold cloth on her forehead. She wanted to go to sleep, but her mind wouldn't let her.

The last twenty years seemed to evaporate into thin air and she was once again a young girl madly in love. Her pulse was racing and her heart beating wildly. She didn't care if she was hallucinating or not. This was the happiest she had been in a very long time. Brent, precious Brent, was alive, breathing, talking, and touching her forehead. She hoped she would never wake up. *Oh, please God,* she silently prayed, *let this, whatever it is I'm having, last awhile.*

As she studied his face, his eyes, his lips, something kept nagging at her. Then it dawned on her. This wasn't a dream at all. Brent really was alive! His once blue-black hair was totally silver on the sides, making him quite distinguished looking. There were small lines around his eyes and lips, crow's feet, a lot like her own. The biggest difference in his appearance, though, was his eyes. She remembered their icy blue color, always warm and laughing when he had looked at her. Not so now. The light silver blue gave her chills at the emotionless way he was now studying her.

Once again she focused on his voice, calling her name. She wanted to sit up and wrap her arms around him. Reason was lowly starting to break through her foggy brain, however, and suddenly she knew without a doubt that he was the reason for her being here. She didn't understand why, but her instincts told her to be wary of him. "Les?" Again, he spoke her name.

Not able to be silent another minute, Les willed her mouth to say something. "Brent," was all she could get out.

"Yes, Les, it's me. Does it hurt bad?"

"Yes," was her only answer as she closed her eyes once again, willing the banging pain in her head to go away.

"Les, I'm going to give you something to ease off the pain, okay?" asked Brent.

Les tried nodding her head, but it was too much of an effort. Feeling a prick, she opened her eyes in time to see a young woman removing a needle from her arm.

"It's a mild pain reliever. Don't worry, I'll be right here," her Brent reassured, as she closed her eyes one last time before succumbing to the blessed relief from pain.

In the next compound, Ned and Dan were dealing with another kind of anguish. It had been a full day since they had talked to or seen Les. Every time the door opened to their cells, they asked about her, only to receive silence or a smirk from their so-called jailers.

They seemed to be the only people in this building, and they weren't hindered in any way from talking to one another. This in itself amazed the brothers. They still had no inkling as to why they had been brought here. They had discussed many times, in the course of the last few years, the possibility of being killed, but this made no sense to them. In fact, they were bewildered why no one had even come to their cells and questioned them. All they could do was wait; and as it turned out, this was the hardest thing in the world for them to do.

Brent was pacing the floor as he watched Les sleep. When they had brought her in yesterday, blood dripping from the wound on the back of her head, he had nearly lost it. Twenty years had passed, but he realized the feelings he had thought dead were evidently still very much alive.

He could remember a much younger Les seeing him off at the airport, the excitement of the plans to get married as soon as he was settled into his new appointment. He'd wanted to be transferred to the States, but he had been totally unprepared for the full schedule of events he had to keep. The first few days had been spent being chauffeured around the laboratory and plant where he would be working, while the nights were filled with PR dinners and briefings. Before he knew it, a week had passed.

He had tried to phone Les, but found her phone had been disconnected. When he rang her office, he was told that Les had left their employment and they didn't have any idea where she had gone. When he phoned her brother's house, he was told she had gone to the States to live with her brother Zack and his wife. They also told him that her fiancé had been killed in a plane crash and she had gone there to try and get her life back together. Hurt and angry, he had hung up without leaving his name or any message.

He still felt the bitter anguish he had felt at her betrayal. How could she have led him on, while all the time she had been planning to marry someone else. To keep his sanity he had put her completely out of his mind and concentrated solely on his career. There had been several women through the years, but Brent would not let himself be hurt like that again. Now, here she was, more beautiful than ever. He had never expected to see her again until B had mentioned to him that she was the chemist the company had to have to help him. He had fought tooth and nail against it, especially when the entire plan was unfolded and he realized she would be brought here against her will. He had no idea, however, that her companions were her brothers. He hadn't seen either of them yet and hadn't been told of their involvement in this matter. He only knew what B wanted him to know.

Being well aware of the disastrous situation they were now facing with Protoan Q, he knew they had been right in bringing Les here; he only wished it weren't under these circumstances. She was a brilliant chemist and had been the original research partner with him on the Protoan project. This fact alone would be unmeasurably beneficial to finding the answer in a much shorter time frame.

He had never thought the tests that had been done in the last twenty years couldn't be reversed. But he had been working day and night for so long now—he could no longer remember—to find some antidote for this chemical, and it had proven to be more than he was capable of. After he'd begged for help, B had mentioned Les as the logical solution. The state department and Australian government had kept the animal killings secret as far as he knew. Thank God the deaths had only been to animals so far. He was well aware, though, that without something to counteract Q, as they referred to it, the human population closest to the test site would soon be affected. Hopefully, Les could agree to help him with this. He just couldn't understand why they had had to kidnap her and her brothers.

That wasn't his concern anyway. He just wanted to get Les on her feet and get started on the antidote. The brass could explain the seriousness of the situation to her at that point. So he settled back down in the chair next to her bed and waited for her to rouse again.

Brent was unaware of the actions of his superiors or, for that matter, the real and total use of Protoan Q. He would have been horrified if he'd known the full implications of his and Les's research and invention of Protoan Q. They had put together this powerful chemical for the supposed use of controlling the overpopulation of outback greenery and wildlife. Only the strongest of the wildlife would survive;

therefore, the offspring of these animals would have a natural antidote born into their genes, resulting in a far superior strain of animal and plant life. So far, however, none of the test animals had survived, which meant no offspring and, therefore, no antidote. Years of extensive research and experimentation had been wasted. Nothing worked. Brent was at his wit's end.

XXI

Bradbury Bingham was a huge specimen of a man. Standing six foot, eleven inches tall and weighing 310 pounds, he dwarfed most people. As a child, his family had called him B.B. (Big Brad) and in his high school years, he had shortened the nickname to just B. He was an excellent athlete and had played pro basketball for a short two years when he had broken his leg, causing a slight limp, hardly noticeable, but enough of an injury to keep him from playing anymore.

His second love had been biogenetics; so when his athletic career came to an abrupt end, he'd devoted all his time and energy into this field. The government had grabbed him up on contract and after a few years, realizing his potential, made him the number-one man in control of the whole biogenetic research division. This position, coupled with his size, made most people keep out of his way.

At the moment he was in an agitated state The men had come back yesterday afternoon empty handed. All three had been severely reprimanded and transferred to the testing location. He knew that without the girl, Penny, his hopes for an antidote were nonexistent and he would have trouble with Lesley.

Ah, Lesley, the one woman who had rejected his love. He had watched her all these years, unseen, through his agents and frequent personal trips he had made himself. After she had spurned his attentions toward him, he had no difficulty using her as a guinea pig, just as he had countless others in the past. She had become enamored with Brent and that suited his purposes well. He had administered small doses at a time to both of the lovers of the experimental chemical Protoan Q. According to their research on this chemical, any offspring would automatically have the antidote in its immune system. The only catch was that it would take until the child matured into adulthood for the antidote to be fully developed. Through routine blood testing done in all the laboratories, supposedly for drug use control, he had known well before Les that she was pregnant.

At that point he had decided to separate the two chemists, thus the transfer of Brent and the story of the plane crash. He had expected Les to stay at her job and raise the child under their close scrutiny. She had surprised him, however, when she suddenly departed for the United States. A plan could not be generated in time to keep her here, so B had had to monitor her pregnancy and the baby's growth long distance.

Several tests had been conducted through the years with one unknowing person after another. All of these unauthorized experiments had resulted in the people dying. They'd suffered long, painful deaths, which closely resembled cancer. In each of the cases, cancer *had* been named as the cause of death, therefore keeping the experimental testing secret.

B had come up with the ingenious plan of using Polly MaGrath as one of these experimental hosts. It had been an easy way to get rid of Penny's adopted mother, but the father had been another thing altogether.

Zack MaGrath had worked for the defense department as an agent for thirty-five years, using the cover of being an author to explain his travels and long absences. After his wife's demise, he had suddenly left the agency and relocated, making observance of the child much harder. Les had also moved in with them, and that had introduced another hitch to getting the girl.

When they had finally caught up with them, B found out that inquiries into his experiments were being conducted. Zack was the most likely person behind these inquiries. He knew Zack had to be eliminated but how was the crucial question. This man was schooled and experienced in all the modern techniques used by the government.

When the girl had turned twenty, B had ingeniously plotted an elaborate plan to get rid of Zack. But before they could act on it, Zack had suddenly died. B had been elated. Now only one obstacle was left.

He could have jumped for joy when he heard the news that Les and her child were coming to Australia. This brought them onto his turf. The rest was pretty simple. He hadn't anticipated Les joining her brothers in their research though. This had complicated his plans. The brothers were no problem. He knew Ned was good in his research, but he did not fear discovery from him. Les, on the other hand, would in all probability recognize the Protoan Q formula she had helped discover and they had been experimenting with. He had planned to take Les and the brother hostage, kidnap Les's daughter and bring her here, thus forcing Les to allow the tests and help with the antidote or see her brothers and child die.

"Those bumbling fools!" he spat for the umpteenth time. He would have to use his man Kurt to find the girl, but until then Les would have to be led to believe they already had her.

Weak, heartsick Brent, he thought to himself. It hadn't taken much convincing to get him to go along with his scheme. The man was still in love with Les after all these years. A genius in his work, but soft, much too soft. He had hesitated when he was told she would be brought in against her will, but he had been easily convinced this was the only way to keep the experiments secret.

136

The idiot still thinks we only use plants and animals in this research, B thought laughing to himself. *Little does he know that he and Les are the only two human beings with Q injected into their bodies who are still living.* That presented a puzzle to him. He knew, though, that they were both too valuable to harm.

Q had been invented as a weapon of chemical warfare. For the government to get its full benefit, though, testing had to be done on plant and animal life. B had been given the okay for this experimentation, but he had taken the initiative to conduct these tests on humans himself. The actual plan had been to use the chemical on the plants that were ingested by the animals. Only the strongest and healthiest would survive. Their offsprings' bodies would develop the antidote as they matured, thus generating a whole new healthier breed. The chemical could then, and only then, be used on humans in this safe dosage. The antidote would be available from the animals for those who had had reactions to the experimental chemical. All the animals, however, were dying before they could bear young. Instead of the chemical slowly dissolving and disappearing, it seemed to be absorbed into the genetic fiber of the plants, becoming more and more lethal to the animals.

B had taken matters into his own hands when he first experimented on Les and Brent. Using very low doses in their food, he had introduced it to their bodies. He had done the same thing with several others, but the outcome of those experiments had proven lethal. It was now imperative to cultivate the antidote. Blood and samples had to be taken from Penny. The samples would have to come from her bone marrow and liver. The antidote could then be made. The only regret he had with his experimentation was that it had drifted from plant life into the water table. Several wells were now contaminated by the chemical. He wasn't worried what this meant to the people; he knew that if the

Pentagon heard of this, though, his days as number one would come screeching to a halt.

This had to work. Les had to help. She and Brent were the only qualified chemists to handle the testing. *When her usefulness is over,* B thought smiling, *I'll take care of Little Miss Priss myself.*

XXII

Penny was about to go stir crazy. Not used to being confined for any long periods of time was taking its toll on her sanity. It had been two days now and still no one had come down to get them. Aunt Martha had sent Ben out this morning to find Devin, only after discussing it at length with the little man. He hadn't wanted to leave them here without protection and Martha wasn't feeling too good either, but she had been able to convince him to leave and find out what was going on.

The hours went by slowly. Penny had just finished her second book and was looking for another. She glanced over at her sleeping aunt and was concerned for her well-being. Food wasn't staying down and she was running a low fever. At first they had thought maybe it was the food. Nothing had happened to Penny or Ben, however, so that theory was thrown out. Penny hoped her Aunt Martha would recover soon and did what she could to make her aunt more comfortable. The time went by much faster when Aunt Martha was telling stories of her dad's past to her. She settled in once again in the corner of the big couch and started reading.

After several hours she looked up and over at her aunt, who was pale and appeared to be sweating profusely. Penny jumped up and went over to the bed.

"Aunt Martha, wake up," said Penny, as she gently shook her aunt's arm. Martha stirred and slowly opened her eyes.

"I'm mighty sick, hon," she managed to say. "Hope Ben comes back soon. Here, help me sit up."

Penny put her arm around Martha's shoulder and helped her to a sitting position, propping the three pillows up behind her.

"Thank you, child," said her aunt, a small smile curving her soft features.

Penny poured a glass of water and brought it over to her aunt.

"I think I'd rather have a soda. I'm thinking maybe the water could be making me ill. I know it's not bothering you and Ben, but maybe my system is not able to digest it or something."

Penny shrugged her shoulders. She certainly didn't know what could be making her aunt sick, but it wouldn't hurt to try anything. Pouring the water back into the jug, she then opened a Coke for her aunt.

"Boy, that's good. I can feel it clear down to my toes." Penny had to laugh at her aunt's comic illustration of her words as she wiggled her toes.

"Hopefully, you'll be able to keep this down. God knows you need something to stay in your stomach."

"Child," laughed Martha, "I could stop eating for a month or two and not starve to death."

Both women laughed at Martha's attempt at joking. Penny took it as a good sign, however, seeing her aunt's sense of humor returning. Feeling braver after the Coke seemed to settle well, Martha asked for some soup.

"I'd get it myself, but I don't think I'm strong enough to get out of bed."

"Quit apologizing. I'm glad to do it. I'll be in a straitjacket before long if someone doesn't find us soon."

"Don't worry, dear. Ben will find out what's going on. We're in no danger down here, and the food supply is good for at least a couple of months; although, I sure hope myself that we aren't down here much longer.''

Penny fixed the soup in no time and had it on the lap tray in front of Aunt Martha. Watching her aunt slurp the soup from the spoon reminded her of her mother when she was sick. Penny would sit on the bed and watch her eat. They would talk and laugh. It was sort of their time of the day. The thought brought a smile and a faraway look in the girl's eyes.

"Penny for your thoughts, Penny," said her aunt.

"Oh, I was just thinking of Mom," said the girl, brushing away the tears gathering in her eyes. "You reminded me of her when she was sick. I used to fix soup, sandwiches, and other easy things for her to eat. At first it was a novelty, and we used to talk a blue streak while she nibbled at her food. Later, when she got so sick, it was dreadful to watch her trying to eat just to appease me. I'd feel bad at forcing her to do that. Eventually, I hated carrying the tray. Dad took over that task toward the end. I just couldn't handle her choking and forcing it down."

Penny looked up at her aunt. "I had forgotten that time until now. It was really the only time Mom and I talked to each other, you know. It was important to me. I'm glad I remembered that." Penny went over to the bed and took the empty bowl and tray from her aunt. Removing the pillows, she helped her to once again lie down. In just a moment she could hear Martha's slow, steady breathing. Maybe now, with a little nourishment, her aunt would get well.

Penny washed up the couple of dishes and sank back down on the couch. She wished for the hundredth time she had been closer to her mom. *Stop it!* she told herself. *Going back is stupid. You can't change a thing.* Pushing the memory to the back of her mind, she reopened her book and continued reading where she'd left off. In just a few minutes, her head dropped to the back of the couch and she too was asleep.

Ben had a hard time going out the tunnel. It was filled with debris from various animals and rodents. After reaching the end, he carefully removed the rock door from the exit. It was still a little dark, as the sun had not come up yet. For that he was grateful. Slipping outside the tunnel, he pushed the door back in place.

From the outside it looked like the rest of the landscape. He was pleased to see the camouflage effect. Softly he moved across the yard to the back of the house. Looking all around, he noticed no one. The backdoor was pulled shut, so he moved toward the front of the house. He then saw the man standing on the side of the porch, smoking a cigar. He was leaning on his side facing the front. Ben silently backed up. That route was now closed to him. No other way but to go the long way around through the woods. It would take him two days by foot to reach Dan's. He didn't like leaving Mrs. MaGrath as sick as she was. He remembered Miss Angela. The symptoms were the same. She would get better before she got worse, of that he knew. Maybe before she got too sick, a cure could be found. He'd see the medicine man about it. He was now a Christian and believed in praying and God, but it never hurt to have a backup. Swiftly, he moved through the woods, his mistress' well-being the sole inspiration for his trip.

The man leaning against the house turned quickly. Seeing nothing amiss, he propped once again on the porch. *I'll be glad when they find this girl,* he thought. *This place gives me the creeps.*

XXIII

Kurt couldn't believe his good fortune when he was summoned by Megan. He had been trying to put together a good, plausible story to convince Devin to get him to help find Penny and voila, no sweat. B would appreciate the irony of the situation. He had been working for AUS labs for eight years now. The pay was good, the work relatively easy. His only job until now had been relaying information to B about the MaGrath family movements.

It hadn't been hard getting them to trust and have confidence in him. His background had helped him fit right in, as he had been raised in the outback on a sheep ranch. He had entered the service, specializing in special forces and undercover operations, until the government had sent him to B at AUS. He had had to laugh at this assignment. His reason for joining the service had been to get away from the ranch, and look what he was doing. It wasn't so bad. The MaGraths treated him like family, which made his job so much easier. He hoped the outcome of this mission would enhance his standing in the service, resulting in a good promotion. He was ready for someone else to handle the field work. He had high aspirations and was willing to do anything to obtain them.

B had given him the whole situation about Les, Dan, and Ned. Penny was supposed to be picked up at the house in the middle of the night. Easy job. How it had been so badly bungled he had no idea. He wouldn't fail, of that he was confident. Watching the attachment Devin and Penny had for each other had amused him. There was no time in his work for this kind of folly. He used women then left. No attachments and no complications. Well, this time it would work in his favor. The success of this mission would depend on his resourcefulness and Devin's desire to find Penny. After delivering the girl to AUS, his work here would be done and he could go on to better things. It wouldn't be soon enough for him.

Devin awoke with a start. Looking over at the clock on the nightstand, he saw that he had been asleep for a total of three hours. Not a long time, but enough to refresh him. He jumped out of bed and into the shower then changed into clean clothes. When he got to the stairs, Kurt was on his way up to wake him.

"Is everything ready?" he asked his foreman.

"Sure thing, Boss," was Kurt's reply. "You feeling better?"

"Yeah. Myree was right. I was dead on my feet, but I feel a lot better now. You have any idea where to look first?"

"I think we should start by going back to Ned's," was Kurt's ready reply.

Seeing the surprise in his boss's expression gave him the opening he was looking for. "I know you think Penny has been taken by the same people who probably have Les, Ned, and your dad." Pausing when he saw Devin's nod, he then continued. "I don't think that's the case at all, Dev. Think about it. Martha would certainly put up a good fight, and it would really be hard to trap that man servant, what's his name? Ben? No. I think they're hid somewhere on the grounds. We just have to look closer than you had time to. If we don't find anything then, well, we can take a different plan of action at that point."

Devin could see the logic in what Kurt was saying. He had to admit that he had been too upset and eager to get help to conduct a close search of Ned and Martha's house. Angela had hinted at a secret hiding place when they were kids, now that he thought about it. She never would disclose, however, just where it was. He remembered threatening her with various child tortures, but to no avail. She was always more afraid of what her mother would do to her if she told. Kurt was right; maybe they were right there in the house.

His spirits somewhat lightened by this thought put Devin in a much better frame of mind and he was ready to go. Myree was waiting at the bottom of the stairs.

"Be careful, Devin," she said, as she gave him a big hug. Once again she faced the torment of seeing a man she had helped raise leave for a dangerous situation. She was a strong woman, however, and she knew Devin did not need a whimpering, tearful sendoff. So with an iron will, she held back the tears and watched him leave with Kurt and Megan. She felt good about Megan helping; but even though Kurt had proven on several occasions his apparent loyalty to the family, she still didn't fully trust him. *Oh, pooh. You're just a worrisome old woman,* she told herself, as she went back inside.

The ride back to his uncle's place took much longer than Devin had the patience for. They had decided to go back by Jeep and, if they found nothing, to transfer their gear to horses at Ned's. Horseback traveling at that point would make more sense in the outback. Devin's mind was going round in circles. Praying that Kurt was right, he was also chastising himself for not having taken the time to search the house closer before leaving. *What if they're hurt or dying?* he asked himself over and over. But there was nothing he could do about it at this point and time.

He then concentrated on where they might have built a secret hideaway, if, indeed, it was not just a figment of Angela's overimaginative mind.

Hearing a voice broke Devin's train of thought as he realized Megan was asking him a question. They had not discussed all that he had found at the campsite before he had gone to bed. Now they spent the rest of the trip analyzing the implications of his findings there.

Kurt was pleased that no trace of AUS's involvement had been left there and, after lengthy questioning, was convinced Devin had no idea what was truly going on. *This will make it much easier for me,* he thought, *to persuade Devin and Penny, once she is found, to follow him to the AUS compound and into B's arms.*

They reached the perimeters of Ned's homesite midafternoon. Deciding it would be best to hide the Jeep and go the rest of the way on foot, they all carefully approached the house. Kurt was the first one to see the lookout on the front porch. Signaling to Devin, he slipped to the side of the house and silently crept up on the man. Caught by surprise, the lookout turned around too late to ward off the blow from Kurt's hard fist. He slumped to the floor. Kurt motioned for Devin and Megan to come on in. After the lookout was tied up and gagged, they dragged his unconscious body inside. Assessing the ramshackle appearance of the hall and living room proved once again a very thorough search had already been performed.

Devin started calling Martha's and Penny's names. He then stopped and listened. Nothing, not a sound. He repeated his call. Again nothing. The only thing to do now was go room to room and search every nook and cranny. So the threesome started in the kitchen and slowly made their way back to the living room. It pained Devin to see the destruction of Ned's bookcase. He was so proud of that particular piece of furniture and the books his brother Zack had written, which were thrown haphazardly around the room.

Putting these thoughts aside, he, Kurt, and Megan slowly made their way around the room. Every board on the wall was checked for hollowness. The floor was searched for a possible trap door. When the living room search was completed, they moved on back to Martha's and Ned's bedroom. Here it was evident that the search had been most intense. The mattress and box springs had been ripped from the bed. The huge frame looked quite naked standing by itself. Slowly and intensely the threesome examined the walls and floor. When they got to the wall in back of the bed frame, it took all of them to move the frame to the other side. It was curious to Devin that a wire was hanging down one poster of the bed. When pointed out to Kurt, the foreman dismissed it as an antenna for the radio on the nightstand by the bed. After close scrutiny, and banging every board on the wall, they still came up empty.

Ned would have been proud, if he had been there, of his and Ben's work. They had anticipated the walls being searched for hollowness and had constructed the panel with steel inserts to hide the opening. It was clever and it had worked. The closet was the last part of the room to be looked into and was shortly abandoned also.

Devin had started to go up the stairs when it hit him. All he had to do was call Kit. Feeling stupid for not thinking of it sooner, he hurriedly returned to the kitchen. Finding the address book on the floor, he picked up the phone and placed the call.

XXIV

Les looked around at her surroundings. Brent was asleep in a chair by the side of her bed. The room had a familiar look to it, and it took only a few minutes to realize that, except for a few changes, this was the laboratory she and Brent had shared when working on the Protoan project. Her head didn't ache as bad and her thoughts were much clearer. She still couldn't believe Brent was alive, but she was sure he was a threat to her and her brothers.

Ned and Dan! Where were they? Easing up from the cot, she could see that Brent and she were the only occupants of the room. Through the window all that could be seen was darkness, which answered another question; it was nighttime. If memory served her, they were really not alone. Security in this compound was tight. Without even getting up and looking, she knew there would be a guard outside the door. It would do her and her brothers no good if she did anything foolish at this point, so she lay back down on the cot. Staring at the ceiling, the last thought she had had before being hit came back to her. Agent Y, the chemical responsible for the sheep's deaths, was the Protoan project's discovery of Protoan Q.

But how did it get to the plant life and animals unless directly planted by someone? she asked herself silently. Then she remembered Brad. He had always given her the willies when he came around the lab. She remembered how ruthless he could be when dishing out discipline for the employees when they every now and then failed to do something they were supposed to do. He was an ambitious man and cared not whose toes he stepped on to get to the top. She also remembered his several attempts to take her out. It still made her skin crawl to think about it. He had never been nasty or mean to her, but she knew the potential was there and she'd gone out of her way not to cross him. He had to be behind their being here and the sheeps' deaths. The thought of the dangerous situation she and her brothers were in made her teeth chatter and she started to shake. The movement roused Brent.

"Are you cold, Les?" he asked, while putting a blanket across her. "Does your head still hurt?"

"Not as bad," she answered. She was unnerved at the calm and concerned way he was treating her. Making up her mind to play it cool and aloof, she forced her shaky voice to calmly answer, "The shot did its miracle. I feel much better. Where's Ned and Dan?" she asked, as innocently as she could.

"Your brothers are the men with you?" he asked. At her nod, he answered. "Must be in another compound" and didn't elaborate any further.

Then another thought hit her. *Penny! Does he also know about her?* Before she could think of ways to ask Brent questions without getting him suspicious, the door opened and in walked B.

"Well, I see you are alive and well, Ms. MaGrath. I hope the lump on your head won't cause you any more discomfort." Les once again had that powerless feeling looking up at the monstrous man beside her. Not waiting for an answer, B continued.

"I'm sure you have concluded your presence here is not a social one. We need your help in proceeding with an antidote for Protoan Q. As I'm sure you have already realized, we have a slight problem. Well?" he said, pausing to give her a chance to comment as he stared unwaveringly into her bright eyes.

Finally finding her voice, Les started to refuse to help but saw the slow smile spread across his face. It hit her that he wanted her to refuse! Stifling her response, she bit her lip, holding back the retort on the tip of her tongue.

"I see you may need a little nudge maybe? I do think we can accommodate you, my dear. You see, your brothers are getting very tired of their cramped quarters."

Les had a nauseated feeling in the pit of her stomach that was in no way related to the bump on her head. She wanted to shout at this brute of a man, to wipe his smug expression from his face, anything to make him go away, but he continued.

"And your daughter. Ah yes, I know all about your daughter, Les, twenty years old I believe, hair like a fiery sunset, a very pretty young woman. Looks a lot like you did a few years ago. Unlike you, she may even take a liking to me, do you think so?"

Les was off the bed in an instant. "You animal! Leave her alone. I'll do anything you want, but you leave her be, you hear?"

B laughed, having received a much better response to his threat than he had even dared to hope for pleased him immensely.

"That all depends on your performance, Les. The better and faster you perform, the safer your precious daughter will be. Do we understand one another?"

Les nodded her head. She was totally defeated now. She would do anything to protect Penny.

Both Les and B were unaware of the effect their conversation was having on Brent. Daughter! Les had a daughter and had he heard right? The girl was twenty. If his quick mathematical calculations were right, Les must have been pregnant when he left for the States. If there was any doubt in his mind of her supposed feelings for him, that certainly put an end to it.

His attitude toward Les turned hard. He didn't agree with B's tactics, especially where Les's daughter was concerned, but it was nothing to him. His only duty at this point was his job. She would have to deal with this the best she could and without his help.

Les collapsed on the bed after B left the room. Turning on her side away from Brent, she cried softly. She heard the door close once more as Brent, too, left the room. Brushing away her tears, Les sat up and gave herself a scolding. *You can't accomplish anything acting like a wimpy kid,* she told herself. Where was Brad keeping Penny? She prayed her child wasn't hurt. What must she be thinking? Hopefully, she was with Ned and Dan. That thought gave her some comfort.

Something was still sticking in the back of her mind. A nagging dread. What was it? She started remembering the tests, experiments, and hosts for the development of Protoan Q. The one factor that they had been working for was the natural production of the chemical's antidote. Then she remembered. Oh, my God! The only antidote available that she knew of, and which apparently still held true, was the offspring of the host animals. That was the ingenious factor of the chemical. The antidote had to be reproduced genetically. The offspring would be virtually immune to any and all chemical warfare attempts. No other means of counteracting Q were available. They had made sure of that. Implications of this fact scared the hell out of Les. The only animals she had come across were dead ones. It had to mean that B had conducted his own experiments.

Could that mean Angela and Mandy? The idea once again made her sick. She knew, however, what B was capable of. Was Brent in on these experiments too? He had to be was the only answer available to her. Why else would he go along with her and her family's kidnapping. She didn't really know Brent after all. Evidently the plane crash story had just been a ploy to get her out of his life.

She shook her head, trying to clear her chaotic thoughts, but they raced ahead. Who was the host for her to use for the antidote? She could only pray that she didn't know them. She was all too aware of how painful the extraction of bone marrow was and the series of blood tests that were going to be needed for the antidote's research and development. Exhausted from the encounter with B, and her own thoughts and fears, Les climbed back on the cot and immediately fell asleep.

XXV

"Aunt Martha, Aunt Martha! Please answer me," begged Penny, as she shook her aunt's shoulder. Except for a few glasses of water her aunt had roused herself long enough to drink, Martha had been in a troubled sleep. Mumbling about Angela and the terrible cancer, she had tossed and turned for the past thirty-six hours. Penny was near hysteria at this point.

"Please, Aunt Martha," cried the girl as she again shook her arm.

"Whaa-what's the matter, child," asked her aunt in a voice so unlike her own, very weak, and slurring her words.

"I don't know what to do you for," explained Penny, somewhat calmer now that her aunt was half conscious.

"I don't know what you mean, child," said Martha, a little more lucidly than a few minutes before. "I'm just napping, dear. Didn't you just get me some soup a little while ago? I'm really tired is all. Now don't you fret."

Penny realized at that moment just how sick her aunt was. "You ate that soup yesterday, Aunt Martha, and except for a few sips of water, you've been sleeping. I haven't been able to wake you or anything."

Martha sat up in bed and focused her eyes on her niece's face. "Do you mean to tell me that I've been sleeping for a day and a half?" asked Martha, now fully awake and bright eyed.

"Yes, I've been half out of my head," replied the concerned young woman. "You've been mumbling things about

Angela and her illness. I kept checking your forehead, and you weren't running a fever or anything. I don't understand this, and it is scaring me to death."

Martha sat motionless and silent for a few minutes, unnerving her niece again, until she realized her aunt was only in deep thought.

"Penny," said her aunt, breaking the silence at last.

"Yes?"

"I don't want to unduly worry you, child, but I'm afraid I must. You see, from what you're saying, the symptoms I'm having are very similar to those of my Angela's." Martha patted the bed for her to sit beside her, then enveloped the girl in her big arms and comforted her as she continued.

"Now, now, it ain't like I'm fixin' to die right now," said Martha, as Penny choked back a sob. "Come now, you get hold of yourself. I just said my ailing is a lot like Angela's, not that I think I have the same sickness. From what I understand and all those fancy doctors tried to explain to Ned and me, you can't catch cancer. So you see, you're getting all upset for nothing. So hush now and let's look at this a minute. There has to be a logical reason for my ailin'."

The two woman sat still and in deep thought for quite a while. Just when Penny thought that Martha had gone back to sleep, she broke the silence.

"First of all, I never thought Angela had cancer." Pulling Penny back against her chest as the startled girl sat up and looked at her aunt, she added, "Sit still now. I have a lot I wish to say. In the event I become totally incapacitated, I want you to leave the tunnel and saddle one of the horses and ride to your Uncle Dan's for Myree. Do you think you can find his place again?"

Penny nodded her head, afraid to speak, being so close to breaking completely down.

Martha proceeded. "I must caution you now, child, about the dangers of confiding in anyone else, and I mean, *anyone else.*" Feeling Penny's shoulders tense, she explained.

"Les, Dan, and Ned didn't want you to know the full meaning of the experiments they were performing, but I believe you need to know, especially now."

Penny pulled away from her aunt's embrace and turned, facing her. Gathering her courage, she nodded her head for Martha to continue.

"The chemical they believe to be responsible for the sheep's deaths has been around here for a long time. Ned and I believe it is also the real reason behind my baby girl's death." Martha paused a minute, as she wiped her eyes.

"We have no proof as yet, but that is what they're after. And even after they prove the fact, they have to determine who is responsible for the chemical being here. You understand so far?"

Penny again nodded her head, urging her aunt to continue.

"We also believe that the people behind this are very dangerous. Les was especially concerned for your well-being and that is why Devin was left here."

Penny could understand why he was so hostile toward her at the beginning now. She knew how much, through their recent talks, he liked being with his father on their excursions.

"Devin doesn't know that Ben told me about Frank, Ned's foreman. They found him not too far from the house. His neck had been broken."

Penny felt the skin crawl on the back of her neck. She gave all her attention to her aunt.

"Ben tells me everything, and am I glad. You see, we didn't plan our escape until Ben told me this and I realized just how dangerous the situation was becoming around here." Martha paused long enough to drink the juice Penny handed to her and continued.

"You see, Pen, the doctors couldn't tell us exactly what kind of cancer killed Angie. Fact was, they didn't know themselves. After she died and an autopsy was done, this strange chemical showed up that couldn't be explained. Then, not long after, Ned was called by Dan to do an autopsy on one of the sheep. They had been mysteriously dying for a couple of years, but because of Angie being sick and all, Dan hadn't bothered Ned until then. Well, imagine our disbelief when that same chemical turned up. The only hitch in our theory was when your mom died."

Martha paused for a moment, looking at the young girl's face. Apparently assured by the question in Penny's eyes, she continued. "The chemical found in Angie and the sheep was also found in your mom, Penny." Martha paused once again to let the impact of her words sink in.

"So what you are saying is that Mom, Angela, and Uncle Dan's sheep were all killed on purpose! That's crazy! Who would have wanted Mom killed? And Angela? Why her and not you or Uncle Ned or Uncle Dan? This doesn't make any sense, Aunt Martha. What person or, or—"

"Hold that thought, honey. That's right, I don't think they were singled out, like an actual murder, except maybe . . . Well, I really don't know. I think—and by the way, so do Ned, Dan, and now Les—that an organization is behind this awful chemical. We believe it was tested, supposedly for some reason we can't imagine, but backfired somehow. The results are these unexplainable deaths."

"But Mom was clear across the world. She died three years before Angela. How did she come in contact with this so-called chemical?"

"Your dad was researching that himself, child, when he died so suddenly."

"Oh, my God!" cried Penny. "You mean the chemical was in his body too?"

"No, and that's the weird part. By your dad's own wishes, left in his will, he wanted no autopsy. He was in on this research from day one. As a matter of fact, he kept it from you and Les to protect you both. Ned and I couldn't figure out why he wouldn't want his own death investigated. Anyway, after we were notified that he had died, Dan called Les and filled her in on the events here. When he told her what we all suspected, she packed you both up and here you are. Honey, someone wants this kept quiet. I do believe, now more than ever, that whoever they are, they will do anything, and I mean anything, to hush us up. You understand what I'm saying?"

Penny's thoughts were in a turmoil. She recalled the conversation she and Les had had before Les left. *That's why she was so adamant about my wandering off.* Then it dawned on her. These people must have her and her uncles! She might never see them again! Penny admonished herself for her previous childish behavior. With Martha so ill, and everyone else gone, she had to keep her senses and grow up a little. She wasn't a child anymore. Their lives, Martha's, Les's, and her own, might very well depend on her using her head.

"What should I do, Aunt Martha?"

"Nothing at the present, child. I'm feeling much better now, and I think I'll try and get up in a chair, with your help of course. That's it," said Martha as Penny helped her slowly get to the nearest chair. "Now, we just have to be patient. Ben left this morning, no, wait, I'm all screwed up, day before yesterday now, right?" she asked. When Penny nodded, Martha continued, "We'll give him a couple of more days. If anyone can get through and get help, it's Ben. I have total confidence in that little man. In the meantime, you and I will have to devise a plan of our own in case the worst happens. But first, I think a little nourishment is in order,'' said her now smiling aunt.

Penny was more than happy to fix something to eat for them both. Although she herself was not hungry, she knew it would make her aunt eat better if she ate along with her. So she fixed eggs, bacon, toast, and orange juice for both of them. Martha seemed to be her old self as she devoured everything on her plate. After the dishes had been washed and neatly put away, the two put their heads together and planned their next move.

Above them in the kitchen, Devin was becoming more and more frustrated. He dialed Kathy and Kit's number and the phone rang and rang. Devin hung up and dialed the number again, hoping he had dialed wrong the first time. After a few more minutes of uninterrupted ringing, he hung up in exasperation. Damn! He knew they couldn't hang around forever waiting for his cousins to return home.

Megan and Kurt had helped themselves to leftovers in the fridge. Realizing he was also very hungry, Devin followed suit. Megan had put on a pot of coffee and, after they had satisfied their appetites, proceeded to fix each of them a hot cup. Convinced now that the people responsible for his dad's disappearance were also behind Penny's and Martha's, Devin was ready to leave and get on with the search. After much discussion with Kurt, however, the foreman convinced him that it would be better to spend the night, rest, and possibly get hold of Kathy and Kit on the phone later.

XXVI

Ben was on the edge of the porch before anyone realized he was there. He rapped on the screen door once, twice, and had his hand up for a third knock when Myree came into the hallway.

"I hear you. Give me a minute, will ya," said the irritated woman. Opening the screen, she was prepared to give the perpetrator a little piece of her mind when she realized who it was.

"Why, Ben, what in God's name are you doing here? Devin, Megan, and Kurt are all out looking for Martha and Penny. Where are they? Come tell me now," urged the old woman as she led Ben into the dining room. "We thought you all had gone and gotten kidnapped or something."

Ben was motioning for a pencil and paper, becoming more and more agitated as Myree continued to talk.

"I told Megan that Ben wouldn't let anything happen to Martha, I sure did. I was right, wasn't I, Ben?"

Ben nodded and fairly grabbed the pencil out of Myree's hand. After writing for a minute, while Myree looked over his shoulder, he paused, trying to figure out what to say next.

The note read. "Please, Miss Martha is real sick, needs help. No one can come but you. I will take you to her. Very dangerous. No one to know. Promise."

Myree looked from the brief note up into Ben's serious eyes. Devin was right to be concerned. Evidently Ben had Martha hidden, but where was the child Penny? And what

159

in the world could be wrong with Martha. The woman had always had the constitution of an ox.

"Where's Penny?"

Shaking his head and looking around the room, Ben put his finger up to his lips for silence. He wrote once again on the pad in front of him. "Penny with Martha. Come now. Need medicine. Please hurry."

Myree knew the situation was a serious one. There was no one here for her to worry about really. She would instruct the rest of the staff to carry on without her. She was trying to think of what story to tell them when the solution popped into her head. She'd tell them nothing except that she was going with Ben to help a sick neighbor. If Devin and Megan returned, they would realize where she was.

Without another minute's hesitation, she hurriedly packed her medical supplies. She had been the doctor, nurse, midwife, etc. to this clan for many years. Leaving instructions with the staff, she fixed Ben a quick bite, then packed a few belongings of her own. Ben finished his meal in a few minutes and was ready to be on his way.

"We'll have to take the old truck," Myree informed Ben. "The kids took the Jeep."

The truck was fine for Ben. It sure beat the heck out of walking. The two old people loaded their things into the truck, and, after a few coughs and sputters, the engine turned over. Shifting into gear, Ben started back to Martha.

XXVII

Penny knew without a doubt that without medical attention her aunt could possibly die. After their talk the previous evening, Martha had lain back down and fallen into another fitful sleep. When Penny checked her about an hour before, Martha was running a fever and was incoherent. She had tried waking her aunt several times without success. Making her mind up to go herself for help if Ben didn't return by morning, she lay down and tried to catch a nap. After about fifteen minutes of staring at the ceiling, Penny got back up, went over to the stove, and put some water on to boil for tea.

She couldn't believe everything that had happened in the last week. It was like one of her dad's novels. As a matter of fact, it *was* kind of like his last book. The mysterious illnesses. The sheep dying.

"Wait a minute!" Penny yelled out loud. Realizing what she had done, she guiltily walked over to the bed to check once again on Martha. Her aunt was sleeping a little easier and wasn't quite as hot as she had been earlier.

Dad's book, she thought excitedly. He had been only half finished when he had died. She remembered thinking that her dad had to really have a wild imagination to create a story so filled with mystery and intrigue. It was a little out of the norm for her dad, as his previous books had been mostly fact-based fiction, romance, and adventure. This one had more of a science-fiction dialogue. She had started to read it just before they left for Australia. He was writing about here! She was sure of it. She remembered asking Aunt

161

Les to pack it, but she wasn't really sure her aunt had. She wanted more than anything to read it this very moment. *I wonder just how much of this Dad knew about? It's a little too late to worry about it now,* she told herself sadly.

Just then, Penny heard a noise. It was coming from the wall behind the fridge. Voices! A woman's voice, she was sure! Jumping to her feet, Penny nervously looked toward the sound. She realized that maybe the people coming in weren't friends and frantically looked around for something to use as a weapon. Her gaze fell upon the iron skillet. In an instant she was across the room and lifting the skillet above her head with both hands, waiting as the voices came closer. She hadn't realized she had been holding her breath until Ben's face peeped around the fridge and she exhaled. The small brown man hurried across the room toward Martha. Myree was right behind him.

The relief Penny felt at having help was enormous. Myree immediately went to work on Martha. She felt her pulse, checked her forehead, and opened her eyelids with her small gnarled hands, which were extremely gentle in their nursing. The threesome were engrossed in helping Myree and failed to hear Kurt enter the room. When Ben realized they weren't alone, it was too late.

Penny spun around at the strange voice. "In here, Devin," said the smiling foreman. "They're all in here."

Penny rushed over to the entrance just as Devin was emerging from the tunnel. Flinging herself into his arms, she forgot everyone else in her excitement. Megan prodded the two lovers out of the way as she inched herself into the room.

Devin unraveled Penny's arms and tenderly pushed her to arm's length so he could see her face. "I thought you and Martha were kidnapped or worse," he blurted, as his eyes and hands scanned Penny's face and body, checking for any bumps or bruises.

Penny could only stand and stare back, totally oblivious to her surroundings. Her mind and heart were caught up in the sheer blissfulness of having Devin there. Finally, coming to her senses, she asked, "How did you find us? Aunt Martha said you didn't know where this room was."

"Kurt saw Ben entering the tunnel. He just happened to be looking around and was on his way back to the house. Thank God! Oh, thank God," cried Devin as he once again pulled Penny toward him and wrapped his arms around her.

Penny wanted to stay in his embrace forever, but she pulled herself away. She had remembered Aunt Martha.

"Aunt Martha's very sick again, Devin. She's been running a fever on and off for the last few days. She's incoherent most of the time. I'm afraid for her," said the young girl as she looked from Devin to Myree to Ben and back to Myree, making the older woman the focus of her unasked question.

Myree started asking Penny question after question. What had she eaten? Was she taking any fluids? Had she gotten out of bed? At the girl's affirmative nod to the last question, Myree turned back to Martha and started talking to the woman in an effort to wake her up.

While all this was taking place, Kurt was assessing the situation before him. He had already scanned the room for guns, knives, or any other forms of defense and was pleased that he didn't detect anything. He was familiar with the testing done by B and was almost positive this was behind Martha's illness.

Glancing again at the people gathered around the bed, he supposed he should feel remorse for what he was about to do, but that emotion was alien to his nature. It did move him in another way however, and he let his gaze slowly glide across Penny's face and well-rounded form. *What a beauty!*

he thought. Maybe he'd have time later—and a small smile slowly spread across his lips.

Myree was very concerned at the obvious difficulty Martha was having trying to breathe. It was very apparent this was a life-threatening illness, so a doctor would need to be brought immediately. As she turned toward Ben and Devin to tell them, her eyes caught the movement as Kurt eased the handgun from his pocket. Her sharp intake of breath caused the rest of them to turn around.

"Let's not do anything foolish," said Kurt in a calm, deadly voice.

"Put that thing away, Kurt, before someone gets hurt," said a now angry Devin, as he started toward his foreman.

"Stop, right there, Devin. I'm not playing around. Your lady friend here is very important to some very influential people. Research is being done at this very moment that is dependent on her presence. I'll be taking her with me—and yourself of course, dead or alive, whichever way you choose."

Everyone in the room was still. All that could be heard was Martha's labored raspy breathing. Ben's eyes were darting around, trying to locate something to use against Kurt, but Kurt saw the direction of Ben's interests and softly cautioned the man, "Don't even try, Ben. I really don't want to hurt anyone here, but I'll not hesitate for a second to blow you away if the need arises, Get my message?" Ben nodded and lowered his head in submission.

Devin was dumbstruck. He looked into Kurt's eyes and saw nothing of the friend he thought he'd once had. In his place was a cold, determined, steely hard man, who would stop at nothing to accomplish his goal. He slowly, purposely stepped in front of Penny, putting himself between her and Kurt. This action caused the gun-waving man to lose his temper. In one swift movement he stepped forward and cracked Devin across the forehead with the butt of the gun. Caught off guard, Devin had no time to ward off the blow. He staggered a few seconds, then fell forward to his knees. Blood was gushing from a cut across his hairline. Penny screamed and fell to her knees beside Devin.

"You've hurt him! Look what you've done!"

Myree sprang into action, grabbing a towel off the table and starting toward Devin. Kurt held the gun back out as if to stop the old woman, only making her mad.

"Either use it or get out of the way," she told Kurt, who then stepped aside and let her bandage the free-bleeding cut. In just a few minutes, Myree had the blood stopped and the wound bandaged.

"Now," continued Kurt, as if nothing had happened, "if everyone is through trying to be a hero, here is what we're going to do."

XXVIII

B was ecstatic. The lookout had returned in the early hours of the morning to tell him that the girl, Penny, had been found. Kurt had everything under control and would arrive with the precious cargo sometime today. He knew Kurt had rather high ambitions and would have to be taken down a peg or two when the time came. Too bad, really; he rather liked the young man.

Brent had been telling him all along that they needed an offspring of the host to be able to come up with an antidote. Penny was the *only* offspring. He was anxious to get going with the experiment. After an antidote had been made, he had other more extensive experimentation in mind for the young girl. First things first though. The antidote would make him the most powerful person in the world. Imagine what control he would have on the government! The endless possibilities made the huge man shudder with pleasure as he headed back to the lab.

Les was awake and drinking the coffee Brent had brought in to her. She still couldn't believe what was happening. She and Brent had started to discuss the experiments that had already been done when the door was flung open and a smiling B entered.

"Well, I see that you are up and raring to go."

"I want to see my daughter before I agree to do anything," said a now defiant Les.

"You will see her in due time, my dear," sneered B. "First of all, I'm sure you would like to freshen up and get into more suitable attire, along with a decent breakfast, am I right?"

"I'm fine in what I'm wearing, and I'm not hungry at the moment. I just want to see Penny. Please, just let me see her for a moment," said a now more defeated Les.

"First things first, my dear. You *will* shower and change. Breakfast will be prepared and eaten; then and only then will we discuss your seeing your daughter. Agreed?"

Les knew B had her where he wanted and could only agree.

"Good, now come on. Follow me," he said, as he led her from the room.

Les was familiar with her surroundings to a certain extent. Some changes had been made through the years, she noted, but not major ones. They passed the two other labs and continued down the hall. Guards were posted outside of several rooms, confirming what she already knew about the security arrangements here. They exited the building and passed by three other compounds before coming to a halt in front of an office-type building.

"Welcome to my home away from home," said the smiling B, as he gave her a mock bow. A young woman, around Penny's age, Les assessed, came out the door. "Amber, help Ms. MaGrath with her bath," B directed. "Do not leave her alone for a minute. If she gives you any trouble, yell. One of the guards will be here in an instant."

"Yes, sir," said the young girl, as she took Les's arm and guided her into the building.

Les followed her inside and was surprised to see a very homey living area on the left, complete with all the comforts. A large-screen TV was in the corner with what Les assumed was a VCR and satellite dish box. She got a quick glimpse of a radio and phone as Amber briskly walked her past that room to the next. They entered a good-sized bathroom with a mirrored table in the middle.

"Do you need help in undressing?" asked the girl as she pulled a washcloth and two towels from the closet.

"No, I can manage by myself, thank you," said Les, a little more curtly than she had intended. After all, this child was only following orders, she thought, and gave Amber a weak smile to soften her response.

Amber gave a little smile in return, which lit up her features. She didn't understand what all was going on here, but she felt sorry for this woman. She knew B could be nasty and had felt the sting of his hand on several occasions. She didn't want to provoke him, however, and continued getting the bathing supplies for Les. The quicker the lady was out of here, the better she'd like it.

It was clearly evident that Amber was not going to leave her alone, so Les shed her soiled clothing and stepped into the shower stall. The spray of water was refreshingly warm, and she had to admit it felt great against her skin. She lathered her body, rinsed, and then shampooed her hair. In just a few minutes, she had finished. Turning off the water with one hand, she reached for the towel with the other.

"Your clothes are on the chair. I'll be just outside the door," said Amber, as she pulled the door shut.

Les appreciated the privacy shown her. Bending over, she towel-dried her hair, then deftly ran the comb through it. She quickly put on the white pants and lab coat laid out for her.

"I see you're ready," said a smiling B, as he opened the door and leaned against the jamb. "Come along, breakfast is waiting," he said, holding out his hand.

Les ignored his attempt at gaiety and his outstretched hand as she slipped past him. Shrugging his shoulders, he murmured, "Suit yourself," and with ill-concealed anger stepped ahead of her.

They emerged into a large dining room. On the sideboard was a smorgasbord of every kind of breakfast food she could think of. Her mouth started to water as she realized how hungry she was. Brent was already seated and so was Amber. Several other men were eating, but Les didn't recognize any of them. A plate was put in her hands by a now-scowling B, who advised her to eat her fill now; supper was a long time away.

Les knew that refusing to eat would help no one and only hurt herself. She had always had a healthy appetite and helped herself to the various dishes. She picked the seat closest to Brent, only because he felt the safest to her right now. No one talked. It was the quietest meal she had ever been part of. She likened it to a prisoner's last supper, then admonished herself for her wild, morbid imagination.

B was the first one finished. Each of the others finished soon after and excused themselves from the table. When only she, Brent, and B were left, the latter began to speak.

"Today will be spent with the two of you going over all the notes and tests that have been done, which, I might add, have failed up to this point to lead to the development of an antidote. I understand, Les, that you will need to familiarize yourself once again to the properties of this awesome chemical that you and Brent discovered so long ago." Pausing for the effect of his words and apparently pleased with what he saw, B continued.

"Tomorrow, you will have your specimen and will begin the development of the antidote."

"What do you mean?" broke in Brent. "We have no offspring of the tested animals. Every one of them, without exception, has died!"

"You are so right, Brent," said B, a little too calmly for Les's liking. "This is no animal, but a human offspring," he finished smugly, as he studied Les's reaction to his words.

"Human! Human!" yelled Brent, as he jumped up from his seat. "We haven't used any humans in our experiments."

"Sit down, Brent. Control yourself," warned B. "I've done a little experimenting of my own."

Brent fell back into his chair as if he had been struck. He and Les looked at one another, both realizing at the same time just what B had said.

"Who? When?" they both voiced at the same time.

"Why, who else but yourselves," said the big man gleefully, now very contented with the shocked expressions on both their faces. Their expressions slowly turned to horror as Les realized what he was telling them.

"Penny?" asked Les, very weakly. As B nodded, Brent slowly realized what B was saying. He grabbed Les by the shoulders and shook her hard.

"Les, oh no, Les, does this mean—"

The tearful eyes and defeated look gave Brent the answer to his question.

"You rotten son of a bitch!" shouted Brent as he jumped up and leaped across the table at B.

"Whoa, now," said B, as he easily averted the blow from the angry man. "You and Les would be better off venting all this excess energy on your research. Penny will be brought to you tomorrow for the first marrow extraction. I do not need to warn you both of any repercussions if my instructions are not followed to the letter, do I?"

"I won't do it!" shouted a now livid Les. "You can't make me help you in this heinous experiment."

"Yes, you'll do this and anything else I ask, Les. I won't try to hide how much this antidote means to me, but I won't hesitate to kill you both and do the experiment on your

170

daughter myself in your absence. This won't be the first failed experiment. Life for me will go on. Do you understand what I'm saying?''

Les slumped back into her chair. She knew she had no choice. Penny had a chance as long as she did what B wanted. Brent helped her up and both of them preceded B back to the lab. Once inside they were given more instructions, then locked in.

Les had realized at Brent's outburst that he was unaware of the reason for her capture. She looked up into his eyes and saw her own feelings mirrored in them.

"Les, Penny is mine then, right?" he asked tenderly.

"Yes. Oh, Brent," she cried as she fell into his waiting arms.

Brent was berating himself for being so stupid, while Les was trying to pull herself together for the ordeal ahead of them.

"Where do you suppose they have her?"

"There are only five compounds on the land here, Les. Your brothers are in the one next to B's. You passed it on your way to breakfast. Penny, that's her name, right? My God, I have a daughter," he stated in a bewildered voice, then continued, "She must be in the building on the other side of his. How, I mean, why didn't you tell me, get in touch with me, something, Les. Why did you leave?"

Les looked into Brent's troubled eyes. She could barely breathe her heart was beating so hard. He didn't leave her! He was having as much difficulty in understanding what was happening as she was.

"I didn't leave you, Brent. B told me you had died in a plane crash. I was devastated. When I found out I was pregnant, I knew I wanted your child, but I couldn't give it the security it needed. Zack and Polly raised Penny. She doesn't know I'm her mother and now all this. She's been through so much the last few years, the last few months actually. I'm so worried. Oh, Brent, what are we going to do?''

At the last words, Les broke down completely and let loose the tears and sorrow she had been holding back for so long. Brent reached out and drew her into his arms.

"God, Les. I tried calling everyone I could think of. When I called Dan's and they told me about your fiancé, I didn't even think it could be me. Can you forgive me for being so stupid? I don't even want to think what you've gone through all these years, the heartache and misery. Les, I'm so sorry!'' cried Brent as he held her tight against his chest.

Les tenderly pushed Brent away and looked up into the face of the man she had loved for so many years. She knew they had to get a hold of themselves and figure a way to get them and Penny away from here.

"Brent, we have to think of a way to escape with Penny. We'll have to stall for time, think of some excuse to prolong the marrow extraction. I can't, no, won't do this to Penny. We've got to think of something.''

Brent looked into Les's pleading eyes. His mind was so overrun with all the happenings of the last few minutes. Emotions were fleeting across his face and heart. Overwhelming love for the woman standing in front of him and the daughter he'd never met, fear of what was facing all three of them, and last and the strongest at the moment was the anger he felt for B. All the years of waste. He couldn't dwell on this. Action had to be taken and soon. Drawing Les down beside him on the cot, he stroked her hair and cheek. He bent his head and slowly lowered his lips to hers in a sweet, tender kiss.

"I wish we had more time, but we don't,'' he groaned. "Let's get busy,'' he said, pushing himself from the warmth of her arms that encircled his neck.

He jumped to his feet and started pacing back and forth. "B is no fool. We're going to have to go over the research done for the last few years. You've got to be able to convince him that you're able to go ahead with the experiments and are willing to succumb to his demands. It's our only hope of buying time and developing a strategy for escape. Come on, Les, let's get started. It's the only way to save Penny and ourselves."

Brent held out his hand and pulled Les off the cot. Wiping the tears from her eyes, she knew Brent was right in his assessment of the situation. They would have to be very careful and plan everything precisely to have a chance to escape. Having the man she loved beside her at last and knowing his capabilities and skills gave her confidence in knowing that this challenge could be met.

XXIX

Penny lay still while she studied her surroundings. The room was like a walk-in closet, small, just enough room for the single bed and toilet in the corner. The lamp on the one table made her silhouette dance on the walls as she sat up on the bed. It had been dark when they arrived, so very little could be seen of their encampment. She did notice, however, that the buildings were lined up. Sort of like the army barracks she had seen at home. As her mind became clearer, she remembered the words Kurt had flung at her just before they brought her in here.

"Sleep well, princess, you'll be reunited with your mom and dad in the morning."

When she had looked at him in horror, he had just laughed and left.

I wonder where they put Devin? she thought. The nasty cut on his forehead had bled quite a lot on their trip here. She hoped they at least had had the decency to bandage it for him. She stood up and stretched her legs. There was a small window at the top of the far wall that let some light into the room. A sound caught her attention. Someone was opening her door. Jumping from the bed, Penny backed into the corner. She felt like a caged mouse. The door opened and the largest man she had ever seen entered the room.

"I see you have awakened, my dear. Come, sit back down. I won't hurt you. In a few minutes, Amber will take you to freshen up and then join us for breakfast. A few things will be explained to you at that time."

He stepped closer to her and lifted her chin with his hand. Penny jerked away and tried to go around him. Catching her easily with his left arm, he swung her back around and face to face with him.

"Don't try that again," he warned as he drew her close to his chest. She could feel the nausea rising in her throat. Forcing herself to look him full in the face, she stared into the coldest eyes she had ever seen. Chills ran through her as an uncontrollable shiver ran up and down her spine. B took the reaction as one of revulsion and roughly pulled her even closer.

"I had hoped you would find me attractive; but no matter, you'll get used to me in time." Slowly, purposely, he lowered his head and crushed his lips to hers. She struggled against him, beating him in the arms and chest with her hands. It was like beating on a brick wall. He let her go and pushed her back down on the bed. Abruptly he turned and left the room.

Penny was shaking uncontrollably now. She knew she had to get hold of herself. The key in the door caused her to once again start trembling.

I'm Amber," said the girl standing in the doorway. "Please follow me."

Penny stood up and followed her into a narrow hallway. As her eyes adjusted to the dim light, she noticed that this was indeed a barracks of some kind. They walked to the door at the end of the hall. Sunlight flooded in as Amber opened the door.

They both emerged outside and turned to the left. Penny was studying her surroundings in earnest now. There were several barracklike compounds. She counted four more, plus an officelike building next to hers, which seemed to be their destination. Amber crossed quickly to the building and opened the door, motioning for Penny to precede her into the room. She stepped into the hallway and was surprised to see it looked much like a regular house. They went past a living area to the bathroom.

"Please, freshen up, shower, whatever you want." said the younger girl, as she gave Penny fresh clothes and towels. She then sat down in the chair next to the sink. Penny realized she would have to bathe with Amber sitting there.

"Can't I have some privacy?" she asked.

"Sorry, but I have to stay in here with you," replied a somewhat embarrassed Amber.

Penny noticed a bruised mark on the young woman's cheek. She could only guess how it got there. She wasn't used to having company while bathing, but she was also anxious to get the blood that had dried from Devin's injuries off her arms and hands. As she stripped off her soiled clothes and stepped into the shower stall, she tried not to think about Devin. He was still dazed when they'd loaded into the Jeep last night. After they arrived, several men had led him away while Kurt took her arm and led her to her room.

"Please let him be okay," she prayed as she quickly showered and washed her hair. Feeling much more refreshed and a lot calmer, she followed Amber into the dining room. They were the only ones there, but traces of the former diners were still evident. Penny took the seat shown to her and was a little surprised as Amber also sat down across from her.

"I'm to be your escort everywhere you go," she haltingly explained. "We will eat together, and, starting today, you and I will share a room in this compound. B doesn't want you alone at any time. Do you understand?"

Penny nodded her assent as she studied Amber's face a little more closely. The girl couldn't be much older than herself, in fact she looked younger. The bruise she had discovered, on closer scrutiny continued across Amber's face and under her eyes. The makeup hid it pretty well, but she could tell the young woman was in pain as she watched her trying to eat without flinching. Penny knew she was probably stupid for feeling this way, but she felt a little sorry for Amber. It was very evident that she was afraid of something or someone.

A plate was set before her, loaded with steaming hot food. Not having much of an appetite, Penny took a couple of bites then put her fork down and picked up the glass of juice. She had just swallowed the last drops when B came into the room.

She felt more than saw Amber stiffen, while her own reaction was a shudder. His features were clearer in the good light of the room and she was sure as she looked up at him that she had seen him before, but where?

"Not hungry, huh?" he fairly shouted. "Well, if you're not going to eat, let's go into the living room." He gave a slight bow as he ushered the two young women into the next room.

"Take those seats over there," he pointed out as he lowered his massive frame into a large leather chair. "I don't believe in babying anyone, as you will quickly learn. Kurt has informed me that you are unaware of your, shall we say, heritage?"

At Penny's puzzled expression, he continued. "Zack and Polly weren't your real parents. Les is your real mother, and you will soon meet your real father."

Penny felt as if the floor had fallen in. B's voice was getting farther and farther away and a roaring had begun in her ears. All of a sudden she felt the sting of a hand across her face. It took a few seconds to focus once again on the man before her and she realized he had hit her. Rubbing her cheek, she tried to keep the tears in back of her eyelids from surfacing.

"As I was saying," continued B, "we really don't baby anyone here. Now, where was I. Oh yes, Les and Brent, your real mom and dad, were part of one of my experiments. Neither of them knew this, of course, so when they fell in love, so to speak, you were a benefit I had only dreamed of before that. I've bided my time, waiting for your maturity and now, well, let's just say it's time for the harvest."

Penny was in a state of confusion. Still recovering from the shock of being slapped, she continued to rub her cheek. Her ears were hearing the words, but her mind was having a little difficulty in absorbing the message. Les was her mother. That explained so many things to her. But for Zack not to be her father, well, it didn't matter to her that he wasn't her *real* father, he would be the *only* father she would ever claim. Anger gripped her now as she looked back up into B's face. He didn't fail to notice the change in her attitude and was rather pleased.

"Good, I see you do have a little spunk. I have to admit, weepy women make me sick."

Penny broke in. "I want to see Aunt Les. Is she here?"

"In due time. She and your father are catching up on old times, so to speak. You will be taken to them tomorrow. Until then, Amber here will keep you company. All the comforts of home are at your disposal, and I will be back to have supper with you both this evening." Rising, he started to leave when Penny grabbed his arm.

"Devin, is he all right? Uncle Ned and Uncle Dan, are they here too?"

"Don't worry about your cousin and uncles. They are no longer any concern of yours, that is, unless you decide to be uncooperative." He watched her expression as the threat struck home. Satisfied, he removed her fingers from his arm and left.

Penny felt like she had aged a hundred years in the last few hours. Sinking back into the chair, she closed her eyes. A vision of her Aunt Martha's face came into view. She had forgotten all about her in the last couple of hours. Kurt had left Ben, Myree, and Megan with Martha. He had taken the battery out of the truck and flattened the tires. The phone lines had been severed and the horses turned loose. She knew her aunt was extremely ill and needed medical attention soon. A tap on her shoulder startled her and she fairly jumped out of her chair. Amber was standing over her with a glass of water.

"Are you okay?" she asked timidly.

Penny managed a weak smile as she took the water from the concerned girl.

"Devin, that's his name, right?" she asked.

"Yes," replied Penny as she looked inquiringly at Amber.

"I bandaged his head last night. He'll probably have a headache for a couple of days, but I'm pretty sure he'll be okay."

"Where is he?" asked a now very alert Penny.

"He's in the next building along with the other men."

Penny stood up and grabbed Amber by the shoulders. She was a full head taller than the young girl and a lot larger. "You've got to take me to him," she whispered.

Amber started trembling and shaking her head. "No, I can't! You'll have to wait till B comes back. He'd hurt us both if we left this building. Don't even try. Please, he *likes* to hurt people. Please," begged the girl once again.

Penny dropped her hands from Amber's shoulders and slumped back into the chair. She could see the girl was terrified of B. She would just have to figure a way to get to Devin and her uncles herself. In the meantime she would get as much information as she could from Amber. The young

179

woman was agreeable enough in answering Penny's questions, but it was very clear she would do nothing to provoke B.

XXX

Devin awoke with a stabbing pain in between his eyes. The bandage was still in place, and he could tell it was dry. *Good,* he thought, *the bleeding at least has stopped.* He sat up on the cot and slipped his feet to the floor. The small activity caused the pain to increase. "Damn!" he muttered.

"What's your name?" he heard and recognized the voice to be that of his dad.

"Dad, is that you?" he yelled.

"Devin? Are you okay?" replied Dan.

"Yes. Except for a massive headache, I'm great. Do you know where we are?"

"Ned and I think this is the research compound where Les worked years ago. It was government controlled, I believe. Did you see anything when they brought you in?"

"No, sorry. It was dark and I was sort of half conscious. Uncle Ned, you're here too?"

"That's right, Devin. How's Martha? Did they bring her here?"

"No. She, Ben, Myree, and Megan were left in the underground room. Kurt brought us here. Martha is real sick, Uncle Ned. She needs a doctor."

"Just how bad is she, Devin?" asked Ned, his concern showing in his cracking voice.

"I'm afraid it is real serious. She has the same symptoms as Angela had. I'm sorry," added Devin, when he heard his uncle groan.

"How about Penny?" asked Dan.

"They have her here somewhere, Dad. Kurt was saying they needed her for some experiment going on. We have to get out and find her, Dad."

"You say Kurt brought you here, Devin?"

"Yeah, can you beat that? I guess you really never know some people. He's the asshole who clobbered me with the gun butt."

"Are you really all right, son?" asked Dan, the concern heavy in his voice.

"Yes, I guess my pride hurts more than my head. We really do need to figure a way out of here though. Are there a lot of guards? How often do they come?"

"The routine has been the same since we got here. They come in the morning, two of them. One holds the rifle on you, while the other empties the bucket, which, by the way, in case you haven't figured it out yet, is your toilet."

"I kind of figured that out all by myself, Dad."

"Breakfast is slid through the opening at the bottom of the door. No lunch. Supper is also slid under the door. So the only time the door is opened is when they empty the buckets in the morning. With the rifle held on you at that time, there's not much of an opportunity to jump them."

"Sounds pretty hopeless."

"Yeah, we can't figure out why they haven't done away with us yet. Unless they're holding us to get Les to help them with God only knows what. With Penny here now, though, things may change. Our usefulness may very well be over."

The outside door opened and conversation came to a halt.

"Our breakfast arrives," said Dan as the two uniformed man entered his room and went about their tasks.

XXXI

Les and Brent had been studying the notes of the numerous experiments connected with the project. The extensive testing was complete in every way. The more she read, the higher her professional opinion of Brent grew. She was familiar with the brilliance of his thinking, but looking at page after page of the numerous experiments he had performed confirmed the respect she had for him. They hadn't stopped for lunch and were prepared to work right through supper, until the door to the lab opened and a smiling B stepped in.

"I see you're still hard at work. Good. I won't disturb your progress then. Supper will be sent to you here." He started to close the door, when Les asked, "Is Penny all right? Where do you have her?"

"Your daughter is fine, Les. You understand how important she is to this project, so you can assure yourself that she is being taken care of very nicely. As a matter of fact, I'm taking care of her myself, personally."

Les flew toward the door only to have it shut firmly in her face.

"You bastard!" she screamed, as she pounded on the hard wood.

"Come, Les," said Brent, as he led her back to the table. "He's not going to hurt her, I'm sure of it. She's too important to him right now. Calm down. We can't be swayed from our purpose here. The more we accomplish tonight, the better prepared we will be for facing B."

"You're right, Brent," said a now calmer Les, as she looked into his loving eyes. "I am getting hungry though. Can we wait till after we eat to continue? I really could use the break." Hearing the exhaustion in her voice, Brent readily agreed. "Sure, we have covered a lot more than I had hoped for already. A break will do us both good. Coffee?"

"That sounds good."

While Brent fixed them both a cup of instant coffee, Les looked on. It didn't seem real, her being here with Brent. He was really alive and still loved her. There was so much to be said. Questions to be asked. She realized, however, that the questions would have to wait. Penny was the main concern at the present.

"I pray she'll understand," Les said out loud.

"You mean Penny, right? Les, you've been with her all her life; if she's anything at all like you, there's nothing to worry about. Was she close to your brother and his wife? I know that sounds stupid, I mean, did she know she was adopted?"

"No, we were going to tell her, but Polly got sick so we put it off. When Zack died, I decided to let it go. We have a good relationship, Pen and I. I just hope this doesn't ruin it."

"I guess we'll both find out tomorrow. Do you think you'll be able to convince B to hold off for a while?"

"After tonight I should be ready for anything," she answered, accepting the steaming cup of coffee Brent held out to her.

B entered the dining room, greeting Penny and Amber as he sat down. "Before you start asking a lot of questions, there are a few I need answered, Penny." He took the silence that followed as her affirmation and continued.

"Kurt says this woman, Martha, your aunt I understand, is extremely ill. Are her symptoms familiar to you in any way?

What I mean is, could this be a simple case of the flu, a bad cold, or maybe a virus, for example, or do you think it is much more serious than these?"

Penny was taken back at the apparent concern B was showing toward her aunt. Maybe her assessment of his character had been too hastily made.

"She definitely needs good medical attention," Penny finally answered. "She's gotten sick several times in the last couple of weeks. Each time lasts longer and gets more severe. My mother, I mean Polly," she corrected, "had the same type of symptoms. I wish Kurt hadn't left Aunt Martha there without a doctor to care for her."

"Try to ease your mind, young lady. I sent Kurt back for your aunt and her companions earlier this afternoon. They should be back, barring any problems, by tomorrow morning. Feel better now?" he asked, giving Penny a dazzling smile.

Penny was torn between wanting to believe he was really concerned for her aunt and afraid he had another ulterior motive for bringing her here. Whatever his reasons, she was glad her aunt would be close to them all. After she nodded her head, she concentrated on the food before her. After not eating this morning, she was famished. Grumbling noises were coming from her stomach and the odor of the fried chicken in front of her was causing her mouth to water.

"Go ahead, eat" urged B. "There will be plenty of time for chatter when we finish."

Penny needed no more prodding and piled her plate with the fare before her. Everything was delicious. B was amused at how much food the young girl was devouring. Evidently his well-thought-out plan was going to work.

He had talked at length to Kurt when they arrived last night. After being advised of this Martha's illness, he realized she could be very useful. He knew Les was no fool and would only drag her feet on developing the antidote. He had to enlist Penny's approval of the bone marrow extraction. The idea had come to him after his meeting with the girl this morning. If she thought she was the only source for a cure for her aunt, he knew the problem would be solved and Les would have no recourse but to go ahead with the antidote.

Genius, pure genius, he thought to himself as he smiled at the two young women. What was that American saying? Ah yes, you catch more flies with honey. Feeling very pleased with himself, B proceeded to be a charming and pleasant host for the rest of the evening.

XXXII

Les and Brent had been up until the wee hours, going over the protein-based solution they had developed. Its chemical name was Protoan Q. Mixed with the marrow extracted from the bone, they hoped it would neutralize the cancerlike properties introduced into the subject. Initially, the Protoan project had been developed for a good cause. Used correctly, only the strongest and healthiest plant and animal life would survive and produce offspring with a built-in immunity against virtually all kinds of diseases and man-made chemical warfare. They never imagined the harm it would do in the wrong hands. Brent had berated himself over and over for being so blind to what B had been doing. They had both wondered how many people had been subjected to these experiments. Les knew in her heart that almost assuredly Polly and Angela were in that category. She was convinced now that Zack had been on the track of finding all this out when he died so suddenly. She and Brent felt responsible for these deaths. The burden was almost unbearable.

They had gone over the procedure for harvesting the marrow, just in case they would have to. They had agreed to destroy all the notes, tests, and Protoan solutions as soon as possible, without jeopardizing Penny's and, of course, their own lives. A plan was conceived just before going to bed. Hopefully, it could be put into action the next evening.

Penny woke with a start. Amber was standing over her bed calling her name. "Penny, wake up. You're having a bad dream," she said, as she gently shook her shoulder.

"I'm up," whispered Penny, as she sat up on the edge of the bed. Her entire body was drenched in sweat and her breathing was coming in gulps.

"Calm down, calm down," she told herself. Then she remembered. The faceless man in all her nightmares was B! The recollection caused her to start shivering.

Quickly Amber wrapped a blanket around her shoulders and sat down on the bed beside her. The concern in the young girl's manner broke the barrier Penny had built around herself.

"Amber," she whispered.

"Yes?"

"What is B to you? I mean, is he your boss, boyfriend, what hold over you does he have?"

Amber sat very still for a minute, listening to see if she could hear anything. As she turned back to face Penny, tears were glistening in her eyes.

"He is my father," she answered in a dead voice.

Penny was unprepared for her answer and let out a small gasp.

"Oh, wow!" was the only thing Penny could think of at the moment. "Is your mom here too?" she finally asked.

"No, she died last year," was the short reply.

"I'm sorry," said Penny as she picked up Amber's limp hand and held it in her own.

The younger girl sat still, staring straight ahead, and continued in a subdued whisper. "He used to beat her. I felt so helpless. She was the most gentle person. When she became ill, he had no more use for her. He moved us into the third building, a barrackslike place. We were treated like prisoners. She suffered so much that I was relieved when she finally died. He buried her, no funeral, no nothing. It was as if she had never existed in his life."

Amber turned and faced Penny. "I HATE HIM!" she spat out, and Penny could see the raw emotion in her tear-filled eyes.

Pulling her against her chest, Penny tried to comfort her as best she could. Penny held her close as Amber spent her tears. She knew without a doubt that the previous evening's charm and concern really was just a show for her benefit. He needed her to help him with something, that was very apparent. She would continue to go along with him.

Loathing for the man now replaced the fear she had felt for him, in her dreams and the confrontation with him yesterday morning. Feeling old beyond her years, Penny helped Amber back over to her bed and tucked her in. Still a little cold, she slipped back under the covers. *I'll need my wits about me to be able to deal with this monster of a man,* she thought, as she closed her eyes and willed herself back to sleep.

Les and Brent were led back to B's quarters the next morning. They were having their second cup of coffee when their host arrived, with Penny and Amber preceding him into the room.

"Les!" shouted Penny, as she ran around the table and caught her aunt in a backbreaking hug.

Les pulled away and looked at her daughter, checking her over for any hurts or injuries.

"I haven't touched her, yet," replied B to her unasked question.

Ignoring his sarcastic statement, Les continued looking Penny over from head to toe.

"I feel like a huge tomato you're checking for ripeness," quipped Penny, trying to lighten the atmosphere a little.

"You're all right then? He hasn't hurt you, has he?"

"I'm fine, Aunt Les, honest. How about you?"

"Same here," replied her aunt, as she pulled Penny back into her arms and squeezed with all her might.

"I hate to break up such a touching reunion," B broke in, "but I must. You see, time is of the essence here. There are several things that must be explained, so I felt it necessary to bring you all together to keep from having to repeat myself. So if you'll all take a seat, I'll get on with it."

Directing his first remarks to Les, he talked smoothly, like a speaker in a convention. She could tell he was relishing his power over them all. "I know you and Brent have spent hours in conjuring up some scheme to put off the inevitable. I'm afraid you've spent precious time unwisely." Turning his attention to Penny, he continued.

"Your parents here were part of an experiment before your conception. They were given small doses of Protoan Q over a period of time. You, my dear, are the only offspring of this little experiment. Oh, I've repeated the same tests over and over through the years, but for some unexplainable reason, all my other subjects have died, quite horribly too, I might add. A shame, a real shame."

As he paused to take a drink of water, Penny looked across the table at Amber. All color had drained from her face. She looked as though she might pass out at any moment. Before she could say anything, B again started to talk.

"Test after test has been conducted through the last twenty years to develop an antidote. The formula is no good, however, without bone marrow, *your* bone marrow. So as you can see, I need your cooperation in this." Penny stood to protest, but B had anticipated her response.

"Sit still until I'm through," he demanded, pausing only long enough for her to follow his orders.

"Twenty-five years of research and testing is a long time. Don't even think for a moment of trying to hinder this final step. With this formula and antidote, I will be able to control

190

governments. I will be the most powerful man in the world. Do you really think I would stand for objections of any kind? Your Aunt Martha is in the next room," he stated calmly, "a very sick individual, I might add. Another helpless victim of Protoan Q. You see, without the antidote, she will surely die."

As the meaning of his words sank in, Penny, Les, and Brent knew he had defeated them all. There was no choice now but to go ahead with the procedure. Les felt a feeling of hopelessness. She knew there would be no stopping this man after the antidote was made. So caught up were the three of them in their feelings of frustration, they almost missed the sudden movement at the other end of the table.

A loud crash was heard in the front hall. Jolted by the noise, they all looked up in time to see Amber stand, a hypodermic needle poised above her father.

B's look was one of unbelieving astonishment when she slowly buried the point in his neck. His eyes were fixed on her calm, expressionless face.

"Yes, it was filled with your wonderful Protoan Q. You won't die the long, painful way my mother did, *Daddy,*" she whispered, "but you will know who put you in the grave."

Everyone except B moved at once. Brent and Les jumped up in unison. Penny was standing up when they all heard Les scream.

Penny rushed to her aunt as she slumped to the floor in a dead faint. Reaching her side in the same instant as Brent, they were both concentrating on reviving the unconscious Les and failed to see the man coming toward them.

"Les! Is she all right?" yelled the familiar-looking man running toward them. Penny was dumbstruck as she stood up and looked directly into her dad's eyes. There was a roaring in her ears and she could feel arms around her holding her up.

"Penny, please talk to me," begged her father.

"Dad, is it really you?"

"No, you're not dreaming, honey. It is really me," replied her father, as he led her over to the nearest chair.

Ned and Dan had joined Brent and were helping Les to her feet. Devin was beside her, concern, then relief, crossing his face as he realized she was unharmed. Penny also noticed uniformed men all over the place. She watched as four of them pulled B up from his chair and cuffed his hands behind him.

"How? Why?" she started to ask, but was hushed as Zack told her he would explain everything later. The uniformed men were now leading a very subdued Amber out of the building. Penny felt so sorry for the young girl. She wanted to go to her and comfort her, but she was being led to another room by her dad and Devin.

Martha was lying on the bed, oblivious to the commotion going on around her. Myree, Ben, and Megan were also in the room, hovering over her unconscious form. Penny was jolted back to reality and knew there was no time for delay if her aunt was going to survive. Finding Les, she talked to her about the bone marrow extraction. Les was against going ahead with it, but she knew that without the antidote, Martha would die. Her condition was critical, leaving no time for long discussions. Penny was adamant about being the donor and just wanted to get on with it before time ran out.

The lab was transformed into a temporary operating room. Les explained the procedure to Penny, while Devin and Zack listened. The site for the extraction would be prepared and a local anesthesia administered. A special needle would be inserted into the sternum and the marrow drawn out. Les told Penny that the actual puncture wouldn't be felt, just pressure, but as the marrow was extracted she would then feel pain.

Penny was frightened but knew there was no other hope for Martha. With Devin on one side and her dad on the other, Penny felt a calmness settle over her as the painful extraction started.

The procedure took about an hour. There was no time to waste once the marrow was removed. Brent was waiting and took the precious material from Les. Penny was exhausted and was given a mild sedative. As soon as she fell asleep, Les joined Brent in the lab. Together they worked with the ingredients necessary to make the antidote. It took the remainder of the day and all night for the two chemists to be satisfied with the results of the serum.

Everyone gathered in the room with Martha, joined hands, and prayed. Les then rushed then all out. She and Brent proceeded with the administration of the serum. When finished, they came outside the room. "That's it; all we can do now is wait. The rest is up to the Lord."

XXXIII

B died on the way to the hospital. The massive dose of the formula administered by Amber had proven to be as lethal as she had intended. Les and Brent had also accomplished their goal of destroying the Protoan Q formula before either the American or Australian government could confiscate it.

Zack explained to everyone why his faked death was necessary in bringing B to justice. Penny, Les, and his brothers understood the reasons, but were a little angry at not having been included in the plan.

Les and Penny had time for a long talk. They both agreed that Penny would still call her Aunt Les. Penny felt a little closer to her mom, Polly, now that she knew the whole story. Zack would always be her father, however, even though she did like Brent and was glad Les and he had been reunited.

Devin had not left Penny's side. His love and concern was apparent in every word and action. Penny's love for him grew with each passing day. He had asked her to marry him and she joyfully accepted his proposal.

There had been no real change in Martha's condition until the third day. Penny was in the room with her, when she noticed her aunt's eyelids fluttering.

"Aunt Martha, do you hear me?" she asked, as she bent over the still form.

"Penny?" was the very weak reply.

From that point on, Martha's recovery was steady and complete.

Amber, they were told, was placed in a psychiatric facility. No one was allowed to visit just yet, but the doctors were hopeful of a total recovery.

EPILOGUE

Two weeks had passed and Martha was almost as good as new, up and around and in her glory, with the whole family back together.

Zack had explained the whole plan, starting with his sudden death. He had actually been living in Ned and Martha's upstairs bedroom, keeping an eye on his daughter and sister. The U.S. and Australian governments had been waiting for B to slip up and make the move he eventually did. Up until he kidnapped Les, Ned, and Dan, they had no real evidence of misuse of the Protoan Q formula. They had to catch his hands in the cookie jar, so to speak, to be able to make any charges stick. Zack explained that they hadn't intended to let it get this far out of hand. But when Penny and Martha had also disappeared, it put a delay on both sides, closing in and shutting down his operation.

Dan broke in and told them about how shocked he had been when Zack had jumped his guards and entered his small cell.

"I thought I must be cracking up or wounded, but didn't remember being shot. It took a few minutes for Zack to convince me he was very much alive and not just a figment of my imagination."

Everyone laughed as they visualized Dan's reaction to Zack's dramatic return.

The two governments joined forces in collecting B's files and the evidence of his unauthorized experiments. The compound was dismantled and the personnel either arrested or sent home for extensive questioning. Les and Brent weren't punished for their part in destroying the formula. Under the circumstances both governments agreed it had been the only thing to do.

Kathy, Kit, and the kids had shown up the day after they had all returned to Ned and Martha's. They had become concerned when they couldn't get any answer after calling for several days.

Penny felt in control of her life for the first time. She and Devin were making plans to marry as soon as possible. Zack had given the young couple the house and land as a wedding gift, planning to return to Australia and help Dan with the farm.

Les and Brent would be staying in America, but they planned to get a place of their own. Penny was thrilled to see her aunt so happy.

The day came for their departure. The good-byes were long and painful. Penny knew the days would pass by fast however, with all the plans and preparations to be made for the wedding. With Les and Brent on one side and her father on the other, Penny was finally content. She was full of anticipation and excitement for the new life awaiting her. As the ship pulled away from the dock and headed out to sea, Penny, eyes shining with love and her body encircled by Devin's strong arms, waved to her Australian aunts and uncles until they disappeared from view.